CW01064534

FALTERING

Elexis Bell

FALTERING
The Regonia Chronicles: Book Two

By Elexis Bell

Eager to stay up to date on the latest dark fiction from Elexis Bell?

Sign up for her newsletter on her website.

www.elexisbell.com

From the notes and sketches of Ambassador Olivia Dobovich on the Marks tattooed upon members of Daen Tribe.

Birth

Death

Battle Death

Traitor's Death

Tribe and Family Marks

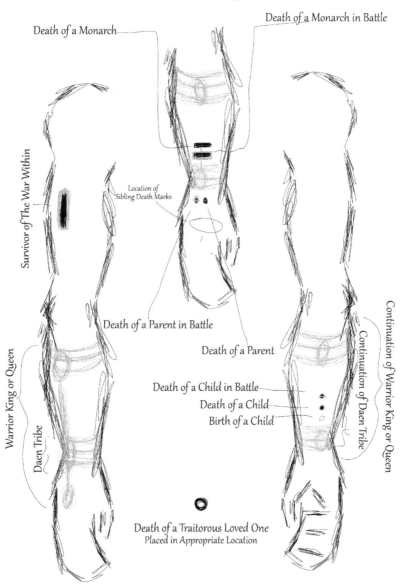

Death of a Monarch

Death of a Monarch in Battle

Survivor of The War Within

Location of Sibling Death Marks

Death of a Parent in Battle

Death of a Parent

Warrior King or Queen

Daen Tribe

Continuation of Warrior King or Queen

Continuation of Daen Tribe

Death of a Child in Battle

Death of a Child

Birth of a Child

Death of a Traitorous Loved One
Placed in Appropriate Location

Partner Marks

Partner
Ceremony

Death
Of A
Partner

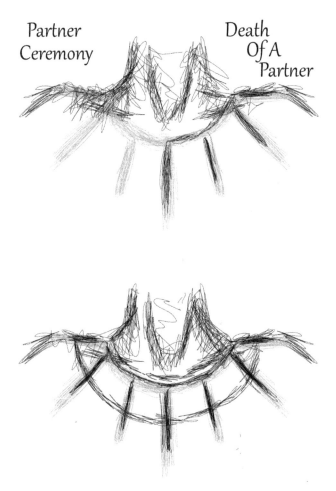

Partner Died in Battle

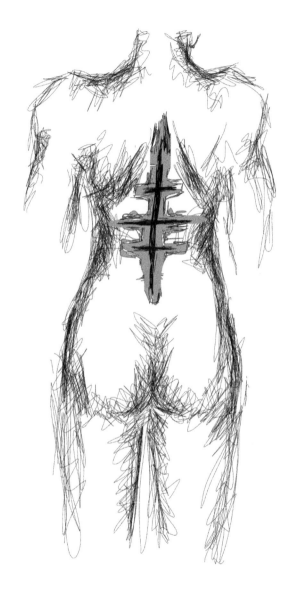

The Awakening

Chapter One
Novay

Reginald

Rone leads me down the hall toward the same room my tests are always administered in. The steel grey walls around me pass in a blur, but my spirits feel lighter than they have in quite some time.

My eyes trace the slender form before me, raking over Rone's wings and the short bob of her hair. She's continued shaving the side of her head, showing pale grey skin to the world even though the cut from her surgery has long since healed. A single braid outlines the top of the shaved skin, keeping stray hairs from falling over it.

A strange impulse begs me to reach out, to put a hand on her arm. My mind floods with the image of her face as she turns toward me, the sensation of reaching out to touch that exposed skin just above her ear. My heart stutters in my chest.

I shake my head to clear it.

Keeping my eyes carefully above her hips, I watch the bounce of her straight, black hair as she walks. I try to push my mind toward whatever test I'll suffer through today now that the Drennar have moved on to psychological torture.

But haven't I suffered enough?

Can't I have this brief moment, this tiny span of time out here in the hall to think pleasant thoughts?

Never mind the absurdity of them, the stupidity. I deserve a pleasant thought or two. Right?

Rone stops after the same 100 steps and three corners I've traversed day in and day out since coming here twelve years ago. She looks at me with worry tightening her eyes.

I gulp back a bit of fear, wondering if she knows what I'm in for today, or if she just has a bad feeling about it. Inwardly, I scoff at myself, still unable to fully believe that she's been modified to possess emotions. But I've seen the evidence myself.

And the look on her face does not bode well for me today.

Turning toward the wall, she sends a command, ears blinking once. The wall slides open, and we step inside. Four Drennar stand motionless, one in each corner, waiting. Watching.

Today, two chairs sit in the middle of the room, though one sits diagonally behind the other.

So she can see me and the scene they've decided to subject us to...

Have they been showing her things, clips of my life or of humanity, aside from these viewings?

A strange bit of guilt flutters through me at the prospect of Rone seeing me with Eva.

If she's seen anything of Eva now, what would that make her think of me? Would I be guilty by association?

Would she turn away from me?

The sensation of her hand in mine, a sensation that has yet to be repeated, reaches up from the depths of my memory. The thought of losing Rone too almost chokes me, though she and I certainly aren't as close as my imagination is likely making it seem.

I doubt she even thinks of me as a friend.

If friends are even a thing among Drennar.

Or... modified Drennar.

16

Before my stupid heart can pursue that line of questioning any further, the lights dim, sparing me. I take my seat, settling in beneath four watchful gazes.

Rone hesitates, staring forlornly at the wall that I know will show me one tragedy or another very soon. Her gaze finds me, brows drawn tightly together. With a deep breath, she takes her seat behind me.

I resist the urge to turn and look at her, but only barely.

A dark cell appears on the wall before me, lined with stone and lit by a fire in the hearth. It looks like something out of an old fantasy movie, but in the bottom right corner of the screen, the words *Ulysses Space Research Station* glow. My brows furrow, and I lean forward in my seat.

"What the…"

An alien, the one from Eva's crate, number 0001, rages inside the cell. Guilt sweeps through me at the thought of referring to him by a number, but I have no choice, have no name for him. Human Guards stand out of reach, faces contorted in anguish.

0001 screams at the top of his lungs, flinging his bed across the cell. It splinters, and the people guarding him flinch.

The screen before me shifts, showing me a new clip of this alien. And now, he sings. Of his home and his people. Of his lost love, Tenna.

But his words…

My cochlear implant translates them easily, having had them programmed in twelve years ago. He sings in the Drennar language.

Yet, emotion packs every word, fills every breath. Pain and doubt and unbridled fury rumble through him, so much stronger than anything I've ever seen or heard before.

17

One of the Guards paces, snapping beneath the strain of 0001's emotions. Angry music blares throughout the room, a thing that shouldn't be possible in a stone cell, a stone cell that shouldn't exist on one of our space stations.

But 0001 only sings louder, shifting his melody to fit the song.

The soldier panics, rushing to the bars and shouting at the alien. He lobs threats of cutting the alien's tongue out.

0001 stands, calm and collected as he approaches the Guard beyond the bars.

My heart stops.

And 0001 reaches out, snatching up the man's arms, only to jerk them through the gaps of his cell, slamming the Guard into the bars.

A cold smile graces 0001's lips as he says, "While I've got you here, how about I tell you a little about myself?"

I flinch as the Guard's shoulders pop out of place, but I never tear my eyes away.

"When our ancestors, the Drennar, brought us to Regonia, it was in hopes that we could live on in their place. They ventured too far into space, exploring places they shouldn't have, and found a strange bacteria that slowly killed them, all the while mutating their flesh. They realized it too late to save their planet. The disease spread to animals and plants alike."

Their ancestors?

I spare a glance at the Drennar assembled throughout the room, but quickly refocus on the screen. The Guard's face pales beneath his tan.

"The next generation of their race was in some sort of cold-storage, waiting for maturity, still untouched by disease,

18

undistorted. They brought their young to this planet, used strange devices to shield them from the bacteria while they taught them what they could before the last of the Drennar died off," 0001 says, sliding his grip to the Guard's hands after two pops signify dislocated elbows.

"Their last words to us before they boarded their ship one final time were to live within the means of our planet, to honor them with our strength, and to find them within the beauty of our own voices."

"We sing to pay tribute to those who have come before us, both the Drennar ancestors who, in death, gave us life, and the Regonians we have since descended from, who forged a home for us on this new planet. We sing to keep their memory alive, long after they've passed, striving to find a sound that perfectly embodies each and every one. We sing to honor the triumphs and the sacrifices of the living. We sing in joy and in pain."

The Guard lolls in 0001's grip, and the alien jerks hard, fully dislocating the Human's wrists to bring him back around.

"If I ever wake to find my tongue gone, I will level this wretched place."

Then, 0001 speaks *our* language, adding, "Do you really think I'm here because these flimsy bars and the four of *you* are keeping *me* here?"

And my blood runs cold.

The wall before me transforms, shining with the bright sterility of a hospital. The bottom corner reads, "Odyssey Space Research Station."

One of the aliens Eva kidnapped lies on a cot. A few others rest beyond her. A short doctor removes the IV from this alien woman's dusky skin, then stands there, waiting, staring down at her sleeping form.

When she wakes, the doctor tells her that her planet was destroyed by a solar flare, that only a handful were rescued, that her amnesia is not unusual. The doctor says her partner died on the trip there, but not before telling them her name.

Tenna.

My stomach turns, knowing that all these lies, all this treachery, every bit of it rests at Eva's feet.

The screen shifts once more, panning over row after row of beds, stacked in the cafeterias of three different stations. All the aliens that Eva kidnapped lie there, unconscious, hooked up to hoses and tubes and wires. The skin on their arms shines around freshly installed Links.

Their vitals scroll on the tiny screens, and the transmitter lights on each one pulse a soft blue, constantly uploading information.

I rise to my feet, jaw hanging open.

"What has she done?" I whisper, voice hoarse.

Behind me, a soft gasp escapes Rone's lips, but I don't turn to look at her, don't dare look away from the horrors my wife committed.

Is still committing?

I glance at the time stamp.

A week? A week and a half? What day is it today?

The screen transforms once more, and I forget my line of questioning.

Because chaos rules the wall before me. Sound erupts, brutal and horrendous, as a small cluster of aliens fights off a battalion of armed Soldiers in the hospital on Odyssey, just below the lab. Their battle rages in a small corner of the screen.

On the rest of the screen, 0001 stands by Tenna's unconscious form, clinging to her hand and anxiously looking at the battle behind him. Music blares across the lab, shaking my testing room.

And then, I see her.

Staring out from a wall of screens, Eva goes on about how necessary this all was, how Olivia should see that.

Olivia!

I scan the wall before me, finally picking up on my daughter, facing off against her mother. But she looks so different, so tired.

What has Eva put her through?

The battle in the hospital makes its way up the stairs, bursting into the lab. Soldiers do their best to take down a handful of aliens, the ones that rested when they woke Tenna.

"Olivia, get out of there, please…" I beg, hand rising to cover my mouth. My heart stutters.

Please, Olivia, get somewhere safe.

But she turns, speaking to 0001, who she calls Krona, telling him to get Tenna to safety.

And the screen before me goes blank.

A wretched scream erupts from me, and I wheel on the nearest Drennar.

"Show me the rest of it! SHOW ME MY DAUGHTER, YOU COLD-HEARTED BEAST!"

Rushing forward, I slam my fists against the unfeeling alien before me, but he doesn't even flinch. He stares down at me, unblinking in the face of my fury.

"Show me Olivia!"

Twin fans of blue light reach out from the Drennar's eyes, scanning me. But still I pound my fists against his chest, screaming wildly.

Arms fold around me, pulling me back. I lash out, kicking the Drennar before me, reaching for him, desperate to inflict some sort of pain, to make that foul creature feel something, anything, even if it's only pain.

But a voice sounds, close to my ear. "I'm sorry," Rone whispers. "I tried to get them to show you something else, I did." Her voice breaks, sapping me of my strength.

I crumble, falling in on myself. My knees give way, tugging Rone down with me.

"Please," I beg. Tears slide over my cheeks. "Please, just tell me. Is Olivia alive?"

My heart shrivels in my chest, dreading the answer.

"Please…"

Rone pulls me against her, cradling my head against her shoulder. My arms wrap around her, and my tears soak into her jumpsuit.

Behind me, the Drennar I tried to pummel says in a monotone voice, "She is alive."

Relief washes through me. A fresh torrent of tears bursts from my eyes, and sobs rattle through me.

Rone puts one hand to the back of my head. A tear drips from her eye to land on my neck.

***

We sit on my bed for an hour, at least. But we say nothing.

I stare at the sleek, blue-grey floor, motionless and completely numb.

22

Beside me, Rone's hands worry at each other. She opens her mouth to speak, the movement barely visible in my periphery. But no words grace the air.

After a few empty moments, she tries again. Not a single sound comes out.

Her blurry shape turns toward me, pulling one knee up onto the bed. Her wings rustle behind her, fluttering over my pillow.

Vaguely, I wonder if they'll leave her scent in their wake like they did last time. The soft, almost floral scent hung there for nearly a week.

Leaning toward me, she places one hand on the small of my back. I close my eyes, unsure what to do.

Her weight shifts, and her lips brush the skin of my ear as she whispers, "I might be able to get a message to Olivia. If you want."

My eyes snap open, and I turn to face her.

I nod feverishly, whispering, "Thank you."

Fresh tears fall from my eyes. My hands move with a mind of their own, reaching out for Rone. Landing on the soft skin of her neck, they pull her closer.

Our lips meet, hard and fast, and her hands find my chest. Our mouths move, hungrily, and I drink her in, wrapping one hand in her hair to pull her tighter against me. She slips her hands up to my neck, touch gentle and sweet.

I pull back, only to sprinkle kisses over her cheeks, dropping one on the tip of her nose. I lean my forehead against hers, warning myself against my own whirlwind emotions.

And again, I whisper, "Thank you."

Chapter Two
Novay

Rone

Reginald's hands pull me close, palms warm against my skin. Tears pour over his cheeks, but he kisses me, hard and desperate.

Heat blooms through me, catching me off guard. A strange fluttering sensation wafts through my stomach.

Suddenly, all the Human movies I watched, all the old recordings of therapy sessions and the notes from them, all the plays and books and dramas I've consumed over the past days...

Feel inadequate.

They didn't prepare me for the surge of emotions washing through me.

But they give me a frame of reference.

So, I reach out, placing tentative hands on Reginald's chest, and kiss him back, savoring the sensations that spread through me. I delight in the feeling of having him so close, of wanting him closer.

My body pleads for more, behaving in ways I never expected, having never really had the option for such things.

Reginald wraps one hand in my hair, pulling me closer, and I kiss him with fresh urgency, thankful that humanity placed so much importance on kisses in their old films. And yet, some small part of me wonders if I'm messing up or doing this wrong.

Hesitantly, I touch his neck. His pulse throbs beneath my fingertips, hammering away just as quickly as my own heart. A rush of exhilaration sweeps through me.

He pulls back, raining kisses over my cheeks. A tender kiss on the tip of my nose lifts my lips into a smile. He leans his forehead against mine, and I stare into warm brown eyes shot through with streaks of blue.

My heart seems to expand, growing too large for my chest.

"Thank you," Reginald whispers.

The smile crinkling the skin around his eyes makes my heart skip a beat, a strange sensation I was sure the Humans made up. Warmth creeps up my neck, spreading over my cheeks.

He's just thanking me for offering to send a message to his daughter.

And I'm just being overwhelmed by strange emotions.

But I know it's not that simple. I've studied these emotions and the effects they can have. I know what I'm dealing with.

They're just more intense than I expected.

He glances at my lips again, and heat rushes over me. A delicate yearning washes through me, aching for him to kiss me again. He doesn't.

Pulling in a deep breath, I lean away from him and try to ignore the desire to lean *into* him.

After all, I'm not getting attached to him.

Inwardly, I scoff at the very notion.

That's absurd. I'm just seeing what kind of message he'll send.

For the first time in my life, I ignore the evidence, shoving away the fact that I haven't mentioned this message to any other Drennar overseeing his experiments. I pretend that it didn't break my heart to see him hurt so much in the testing room, pretend that I haven't been going back over all the footage we have of him.

Needing space to analyze what this means for me, I rise to my feet.

"I should go. You need to rest," I say, doing my best to mimic the flat tones of my kind. "I'll let you think of what to say. We can record it tomorrow after your testing."

Meandering to the door, I focus too hard on how my arms hang at my sides as I walk away from him. They swing awkwardly. I conjure up images of how other Drennar walk, attempting to mimic their movements just to seem normal.

Behind me, footsteps pitter patter across the floor. I smile, and heat floods through me as images from a million Human movies come to mind.

Is he going to grab my arm and stop me from leaving? Is he going to kiss me again?

But he stops behind me, albeit closer than he used to stand.

I reach the wall, pausing as it slides back within itself to allow me passage. I wait for just a second longer than I should, staring into the hall, hoping he'll reach out and pretending all the while that same hope doesn't exist.

One step into the hall.

"So…"

I smile as his voice wraps around me. Turning to face him, I wait for him to continue. He stands with his hands before him, the fingers of one hand fiddling with those of the other.

He clears his throat. "Um… How many massive grey alien races are out there?"

I drop my gaze to the floor, smiling.

Is he stalling? Trying to keep me here?

"There are many races throughout many galaxies, but none like us," I say. "The Regonians are born of us."

"Are there others like me?" he asks.

Another meaning seems to simmer beneath his words, swirling like a powerful undercurrent. Before the surgery, I never would've picked up on it.

Now, it warms my cheeks.

"There are none quite like you," I say, answering both his questions.

I turn and walk away, venturing into the hall. I don't look back, but I do allow myself the privilege of checking the security footage in the hall.

He stands in the doorway, smiling after me, and the image burns itself into my mind. My own smile follows me all the way back to my quarters.

Chapter Three
Venice Space Research Station

Ricardo

My footsteps ring out loud on the metal ramp as I walk with Olivia out of the small spaceship. Dr. Sullivan, Krona, and Tenna walk ahead of us, and the two surviving Regonians from Odyssey follow in our wake, sandwiching us between giants.

My thoughts turn to the third Tribe member that we hoped would survive, the one that succumbed to an old wound reopened in the attack. Her blood fills my mind, and all I can see is the bright crimson waterfall pouring over the edge of her bed as the nurses tried to staunch the bleeding.

My heart twists at the senseless violence, the pointless death. I struggle to wrap my head around it, try to figure out how my own brother, Ferdinand, could have been party to it. But I can't reconcile the little boy he was with the man who could've done this.

Couldn't they have just tried to talk to Daen Tribe? They could've asked about the Drennar, could've talked about battle tactics.

Anything but kidnapping them and experimenting on them.

I sigh, following the Warrior King and Warrior Queen of Daen Tribe, my alien friends, to wake a third of their Tribe. Well, half the Tribe, now. Francis' concerns run through my thoughts, anxious murmurs about Humans being present when 2,000 pissed off and clearly superior aliens wake up to discover everything they've ever believed was a lie.

Oh, and they've been kidnapped and experimented on.

But they deserve someone to be there, someone to begin the reparations, and we can't afford to look weak or fearful.

Besides, we'll have to work together if we're going to make any progress with the Drennar.

I pull in a deep breath as we wander through the halls of an empty station, empty save for the cafeteria turned laboratory, or more accurately, torture chamber.

Tenna takes Krona's hand, weaving her fingers through his. They glance at each other, drawing strength from one another's presence.

A twinge of wistful longing stirs within me, and I glance at Olivia, wondering if I should reach for her hand. Her features droop in a frown, and all the luster has fallen from her complexion. Her hazel eyes stare into space, just as they have ever since the attack.

Last night flows through my mind.

Freshly released from the hospital, I went to her room, accepting the invitation she extended. She gave me the bed, spreading a pallet of blankets on the floor for herself, only to recline against the side of the bed for hours, working away on her computer. She said almost nothing, typing feverishly until her hands cramped.

"Goodnight," she had whispered meekly, curling up on her side when she couldn't type another moment.

I lay awake in her bed, surrounded by her scent, staring into the dark. My arms ached to reach for her. I itched to speak, to ask yet again if she wanted to talk.

But she clearly didn't want to.

So, I held myself still, arms folded over my chest.

Until I heard her crying, muffled by a pillow.

My heart crumbled, and I couldn't hold myself back anymore. I threw the blankets off and rolled out of bed, wincing at the pain from my still-healing wounds.

Nestling into the pallet of blankets, I gathered her into my arms. I tugged the pillow from her face, baring her sorrow. She pressed her palms against her eyes, but I wrapped myself around her.

She turned to face me, shoulders shaking as she buried her face in my chest. She clutched my back, gasping until she fell asleep.

But now?

She holds herself apart, eyes glazed over and lustrous hair limp around her face. Finally, she looks up at me, and where she might have smiled and flirted, she merely blinks. Her gaze drops quickly, watching her feet as they hit the cold metal floor.

Krona and Tenna stop, drawing my attention outward. The cafeteria doors wait before them, but they face each other, foreheads together. They cup each other's necks, eyes closed.

And with every second, they breathe easier.

My chest constricts, and I ache to reach for Olivia, to draw strength from her and offer my own to her, even if we haven't known each other long. Giving in, I take her hand.

She doesn't pull away, but her fingers hang loose between mine.

Krona and Tenna part, turning for the doors. They stand with shoulders back and chins up, every bit as confident as I'd expect alien warriors to look. Clad in stunningly sturdy leather armor, with war axes liberated from the labs that studied them hanging in loops at their belts, they ooze prowess and cunning.

"Ready?" Krona asks.

I swallow nervously, but I nod. Olivia drags her eyes up from the floor, shoring herself up. She and Doctor Sullivan answer in unison, "Yes."

36

But could we ever truly be ready for this?

The two Regonians behind us, an old woman and a man around Krona's age, say, "Toh, Inerans."

My cochlear implant translates, "Yes, Monarchs."

Krona and Tenna push the doors open, and my heart drops. Terminals and screens cast dim blue light over the room, illuminating two thousand sentient beings. They lie unconscious in beds stacked five high.

Washington Station flickers through my mind in jolts of electricity and flailing limbs. Smoking bodies flash before my eyes, and my gorge rises.

But the reality before me isn't much better. Row after row of drugged people, stolen from their homes, lie completely helpless.

But not for long.

I'll set this right.

I'll fix Ferdinand's mistakes, not for his sake, but for them.

I step through the doors, and we begin the arduous process of removing I.V.s and waking the Regonian people. We'll set off for Beijing Station after that, where they'll help revive their fellow Tribe mates. I take a deep breath and squeeze Olivia's hand.

She sort-of squeezes back.

Then, we set to work.

Chapter Four
Venice Space Research Station

Tenna

We remove I.V.s quickly, deft fingers tugging these terrible things from the arms of our friends, our families, our people. I approach a new stack, chest hollow at the sight of a young woman lying still, arm bandaged and face polka dotted with strange little circular pads.

I touch her arm, warm and soft, skin unmarked save the ones at her wrists, which mark her a member of Daen Tribe. The vivid blue stands out beautifully against her dark grey skin.

With a sigh, I take the needle in hand, pull it free, and press down on the little hole left in its wake. Olivia tugs the pads from her skin, lays them on the little shelf that sticks out from her bedside.

She climbs up the ladder, removing the little pads from the man on the bunk above, then the elderly woman above him.

As Olivia moves to the next bunks up, the woman before me stirs. Her eyelids flutter. Her hands ball into fists.

Sitting bolt upright, she gasps, eyes darting around the room. Panic fills her gaze.

I hurry to say, "It's okay. Your Inerans are here. We're safe for now."

She turns wide eyes on me, chest heaving with ragged breaths. "Tinera! Where are we?" she whispers, gaze darting around. She looks down, stares in horror at the flimsy gown the Humans put her in, at the strange bandage on her arm. "What happened? The star-touched came down. Where's my mother? My sister? Are they okay?"

I clasp her shoulder gently, and she quiets.

"What's your name?" I ask.

"Vestaren," she says, voice a quiet husk.

"Vestaren, I have many answers to give you," I say. "But there are many more left to find. For the moment, you and I are safe, but I need your help."

She stills, nodding once.

"I'll explain soon with the help of your Kinera, but first, we must wake everyone else." I direct her gaze to the other beds. "Not everyone is here. Some are in another place like this, so if you don't find your family among these beds, don't lose hope. Even if they aren't here, they *might* be okay. Sit here until your legs will support you. When you can, please go to the other beds, remove these little circles from their skin."

I hold up one of the little pads to show her, and she nods again.

44

"After that," I say, holding up the needle, "gently pull this little thing from their arm. Sit with them until they wake. Tell them your Inerans will answer their questions soon. Can you do that? It's okay if you need to lie still for a while."

She nods, gaze jumping from one place to another, taking everything in. "I can... I can try."

"Thank you," I whisper.

From the top bunk, Olivia begins her descent.

"There is one more thing I must say right now, more information for you to pass along to whoever you wake."

I look up at Olivia, waiting for her to climb down beside me. She tucks a strand of her long hair behind her ear, eyes alert. But the curiosity I've seen in them of late is gone, squeezed out by the strain which tightens her gaze and furrows her brows.

"This is Olivia," I say, putting a hand to my friend's back.

Vestaren stares, jaw falling open as her eyes roam over the alien before her.

"She's an ally," I say. "She helped Kinera and I get to you. All the Humans here did. You can trust them. Olivia, this is Vestaren."

Olivia offers a tentative smile. I explain the translator to Vestaren, careful to mention that it isn't star-sickness and leaving out, for now, the bit about some of the Humans intending to employ it when they found the best means of brainwashing our people to use them as their own personal warriors in a battle that never concerned us.

Except that maybe it does, since the Drennar are alive, since they've been watching us.

At the next row of bunks, someone screams, loud and piercing. It echoes off the walls, and Olivia and Vestaren both jump. My heart rips in two, and my brows furrow at the agony in that voice. I turn to find Krona whispering softly, soothing the young boy on the bottom bed.

Vestaren leans forward, watching him.

"Not everyone who wakes will be calm," I tell her. "If you need to lie still, be strong enough to honor your body's needs."

She meets my gaze. "I will. But I think I can do this. My mother…" Her voice breaks. "My mother teaches younglings. I help her. I'm used to screaming."

A faint smile touches her lips, and I return the expression.

"I must go to the next bed," I say. "Would you like Olivia to sit with you?"

46

"Is there anything she needs to do?"

"I'm only removing the pads, so a member of Daen Tribe is there for the actual waking up part," Olivia says. "My part is quick. I can sit with you."

Vestaren jumps as the cochlear implant speaks within her mind, translating Olivia's words. She blows out a breath.

"Yes. Please sit with me," she finally says.

Olivia settles on the side of the bed, and I climb up the ladder to the next bunk. My heart races, and my palms sweat. But I gently pull the needle from this man's arm and wait.

***

I hang onto the top rung of the ladder, eyes roaming over the beds, the people. I search for my family, reminding myself that I may not be the one to wake them, that they may be on Beijing Station.

Or they might have been on Washington Station.

My heart lurches in my chest, and I tell myself to be optimistic. But what right do I have to ask other families to bear the burden of loss in my place? What right do I have to hope for all my loved ones to survive when a third of our Tribe is gone?

Guilt swirls through me, because despite all of it, I can't help hoping, even knowing they'd give themselves up for the sake of sparing others the loss of their own loved ones.

I breathe deeply, waiting for the man in the bunk a few rows over to wake, the last on this station. My mind spirals, trying desperately to find the right words to explain all of this to our people, to dash all their dreams and beliefs, to tell them everything we've ever known was a lie.

But I can't think of a way to soften the blow.

Especially with so many lives lost.

We'll just do what we always do, what sets us apart from the Human government.

We'll tell them the truth.

Inerans from long ago, before my family rose through our ranks of Warriors and took power generations ago, learned not to anger a slew of Warriors with lies and half-truths. And my family has always trusted our people to be strong enough to bear the burden of truth.

The man a few rows over sits up slowly, gazing around with his face slack. Krona speaks to him, soft words inaudible at such a distance. The man's eyes land on me, and relief washes over him. He looks back to Krona with a nod.

I meet Krona's gaze, give him a weary smile, and climb down. Picking my way through the crowd of seated and standing Regonians, I move toward the stack Krona sat atop.

All around, people sit shoulder to shoulder, leaning together, weeping and whispering. A few cling so tightly to each other that I'm sure they're family, reunited amidst the chaos.

I crane my neck as I walk, searching faces as I pass, peering through the rows. In the opening to the hall, I see two familiar faces. Nearly-black eyes stare out beneath stark-white eyebrows and a shaved head.

Rashka...

My heart stops for just a moment, and I stare at her. She rests her head against Oruta's chest, his long black braid draped over her shoulder.

I sag with relief as I move toward Krona's parents, and I smile when their eyes find me. The people seated on the floor slow my progress, but I make it to them, throw my arms around them.

Rashka's hands tangle in my hair, and Oruta clutches my shoulders, gaze raking over me, searching for injuries.

"Are you okay?" he asks. "Is Krona?"

My throat closes over the words I try to speak, so I nod instead. Tears prick at the corners of my eyes, and I marvel at them, obviously disoriented and confused, but alive.

"Mother? Father?" Krona calls, rushing through the seated bodies as quickly as possible.

I glance up at his awe-stricken face and know that he wasn't the one to wake them. Relief sparkles in the tears falling from his eyes. When he reaches us, he crushes us all in a hug, strong arms wrapped around the three of us, and some small scrap of home falls back into place.

Because even if the Drennar lied, we still have this.

Krona pulls back, speaking softly with his parents, and I stare out at the crowd. I lean into Rashka, sling an arm over her shoulder to pull her against me, even as I search for my own mother.

But my family doesn't surface.

Krona takes my hand, gives it a gentle squeeze. I incline my head, and Rashka and Oruta give us each one last bone-crushing hug before settling on the floor. It's time for us to speak to our people.

I'll search for my family after. Maybe they'll come forward after they see me speak. Or maybe they're on Beijing Station.

Or maybe they're among the dead on Washington.

My heart twists, painfully. A lump forms in my throat, and I struggle to swallow it down.

Krona and I stand near the door, looking out at the people seated before us. In all directions, our Tribe members crowd together, hands on each other's shoulders and legs, leaning against one another for comfort.

Looking to us for answers.

Olivia sits with Ricardo, leaning back against a bunk, and she sends me a message when she's hooked our Links into the speakers of the cafeteria. Krona and I lace our fingers together, and I pull in a deep breath.

I tell them of the lies of the Drennar, their treachery against the Humans. I tell our people that the Drennar have been watching us, tell them that they've been taking Humans.

And then I tell them where we are and why. I speak of the small sect of Humans who abused the power their people allowed them, only to steal us away from our homes, to bring us to this foreign place in the Realm of Stars, to experiment on us.

Sobs mingle with angry shouts. Faces fall, scrunched by sorrow and fury. Whispered questions hiss through the air, riding on an undercurrent of need.

For justice. For the return of family. For our home.

I raise my hand, and they all fall silent, anticipating whatever Krona or I may say next. Their features still burn with rage. Tears still fall, pouring over cheeks of every shade of grey.

But they listen.

And now, Krona takes his turn to speak.

I wait for his words, craving the encouragement I know he'll provide just as much as they do.

He's always had a way with words, be it striking fear into enemies or comforting those in need of hope.

I look to him, eyes softening with pride, and he begins his address. "Rest assured," he says. "The Humans responsible will pay for their deeds. We *will* see to it."

The air shifts around us, moving with sighs of relief and nods of approval. I squeeze Krona's hand, offering him my strength.

"Many of you asked what the actions of the Drennar mean for us. What will we do? Who are we without them? Why bother to go on…" he says, repeating some of their questions back to them.

The faces before us stare on, begging him to give them hope, to give them any reason to keep going.

And he doesn't disappoint.

"We are who we are because that is who we built ourselves up into. They told the same lies to other Tribes across the planet and some on two other planets, as well, yet we are different. Even from Roon Tribe and the Vaerkin, we are different. *They* did not forge our culture, our lives, our Tribe. *We* did."

He pauses for effect, letting a hush settle over the room. Then he says, "We are Daen Tribe."

His words begin to take hold of them. Uncertainty yet lingers in the corners of their eyes, tugging at the edges of their lips, but it no longer has them fully within its grasp.

"We live simply, so as not to destroy that which we depend upon. We sing to remember those we have lost and to celebrate those who remain with us. We dance to feel the energy of life, in all its complexities and variety. We *fight* to protect what we *love*."

Determination shines in his eyes, and his words gather strength as they echo around the room, booming through the speakers. My heart expands in my chest, and tears prick the corners of my eyes.

"We do these things not because that is who we were *told* to be, but because that is *who we are*."

His voice swells, full of hope and purpose. Eyes shining brilliantly, Krona says, "We are Daen Tribe, and this will not break us!"

Cheers erupt all around us, and my heart leaps into my throat. Hope stares up at me from just over two thousand faces.

But weariness tugs at the back of my mind. Because we still have to do this again on Beijing Station.

Chapter Five
Odyssey Space Research Station

Olivia

Maria chuckles, staring at me over the bar after I tell her where the little elephant hides. "I was worried it would be you that found that little thing," she says. Reaching for a full bottle of my Perrin whiskey, she settles it on the bar. "We'll be broke by the end of the week."

I cast a glance at the crowd gathered here despite everything, or perhaps, *because* of everything.

Maybe I'm not the only one trying to forget.

"Somehow, I think you'll be alright," I say, voice too quiet to be heard over the music and the mass of people on the dance floor. Maria seems to understand my meaning, though.

I grab the bottle, but I hesitate. "Can…" I clear my throat and try again. "Can I have another bottle? So I don't have to come back tomorrow?"

"Tomorrow?" Maria laughs. "I hope you don't drink that whole bottle tonight."

Shaking her head, she pulls a second bottle from beneath the bar. "I'm sure you'll need a second by the end of the week, but please… Don't drink a whole bottle in one night. The little elephant isn't a challenge."

"I know," I say.

Her face falls, brows scrunching together as she tries to pick my tone apart. But the music tramples over it, obscuring the nuances, hiding them from her perceptive ears.

"I'll see you tomorrow." I grab my bottles of whiskey and drift back to my room.

My thoughts swirl with images of Lachlan above me, choking me, his blood dripping onto my face, then the twitching limbs of dying Regonians. I wince with each shudder of alien bodies, each insane scream erupting from the lips of a man I once considered a friend.

The halls pass in a blur, and my eyes rarely leave the floor. They don't need to. I've walked these floors so many times, often drunk, that my feet know the way better than I do.

My door slides open, welcoming me in, and I leave the lights off. Kicking my shoes off, I stow one bottle in the trunk at the end of my bed and open the other. I take a swig, relishing the sensation as the alcohol burns the worlds away.

Settling the bottle on my nightstand, I curl into my blankets, tugging them up over my head in the chill of Ricardo's absence. A Guard shift keeps him away, leaving me to my thoughts, and tomorrow floods my mind, taunting me. Dread fills my gut, twisting me into knots.

I reach for the bottle. Sitting up just enough not to choke, I gulp the alcohol down, stopping myself just before I drain it, then stow it away beneath my bed. But everything in me cries out for more, for the relief it promises.

Slowly, the world blurs, and I lie back down. Tugging the blankets back into place, I let the alcohol lull me into warmth and sleep.

***

My alarm screams inside my skull, shattering the peace I barely found last night. Setting my lights to their dimmest setting, I squint at my room, only to find it still empty.

Groaning, I rub my hand over my face. My stomach churns as I sit up, wishing I could stay in bed longer to sleep this off, to sleep it all off.

Why do they always do tribunals so early?

I swallow, throat still sore and bruised from Lachlan's grip. Rising to my feet, I beg my stomach to have mercy on me and my battered neck.

I shuffle to the bathroom, kept deliberately dark so the lights don't stab my eyes, so I don't see myself in the mirror.

Shedding my clothes, I step into the shadows of the shower and attempt to wash away the nightmare of my life. But Lachlan's tribunal hangs over my head, looming an hour away.

I'll have to reveal the monster that hid behind my friend's face for years, have to show it to everyone. I'll have to tell them all that I never saw it, that I was too blind to know who I was really talking to.

And they'll think I'm stupid.

Why wouldn't they?

I rub my face again. The bottle calls to me from beneath my bed, but I refuse its siren call. I can't go to a tribunal drunk.

I close my eyes, thinking of my ship, Sparrow.

I'll fly soon. I'll be in the stars, and my life and my problems won't mean a goddamn thing for a little while.

I set about washing, desperately clinging to my ship and my memories of space. Tears mingle with the water running over me. I dry my hair and dress quickly, fighting the urge to put on a scarf to cover my battered neck.

They'll need to see the bruises at the tribunal.

My cheeks burn, and I sigh, forcing myself out of my room to pick up Tenna and Krona, to fly down to Termana for Lachlan's tribunal.

***

Johnathan Croon, Minister of Human Affairs, and the Honorable Judge Supreme Martine preside over Lachlan's tribunal, a paltry turnout compared to the tribunal looming on the horizon. They sit on a small raised dais, reviewing forms and files on the screen of their table as they wait.

I take my place at one of the tables facing them with my heart pounding. Ricardo comes along with me, tugged into his seat by the hand he holds. Tenna and Krona sit behind me. They grasp my shoulders, squeezing lightly.

But my stomach churns.

The door opens, and I turn to stare as a Guard leads Lachlan in, careful of his cuffs. My heart stops, and again, I see him straddling me, choking me. I hear his hoarse, nonsensical screams.

But the man settling into a chair across the aisle from me is docile.

He sits quietly beside his counselor, and his gaze never rises from the table. Silence descends on the little court room, and I tear my gaze from him.

But I know a monster hides behind those vacant eyes.

I shudder, wondering what else I missed, what other parts of my life are just waiting to shatter.

Johnathan Croon speaks, opening the tribunal. His words fall around me, soft murmurings, but I don't hear their meaning. Judge Martine addresses us, saying something about the bruises on my neck.

Ricardo squeezes my hand under the table as he gives his testimony, but I barely even lift my gaze. Krona and Tenna speak next, and Tenna's words pierce the haze of my mind as she mentions noticing that he liked me, but not knowing if she could trust her instincts on Human interactions.

And suddenly, it's my turn, my time to condemn a man I once thought my friend. I recount everything from the strange looks he gave me when he started asking why Ricardo was different, the fury as he shouted that the rules, and thus my mother, were right.

That night pours out of me, replaying in my mind, and all I can see is his bloody nose dripping onto my forehead as he strangled me. Tears prick at my eyes, and I try to hold them back.

But they fall, despite my efforts.

A gentle squeeze on my hand, a whispered reassurance.

But I haven't felt this alone in so long.

Because if my friend can hide such a monster within, if my mother can murder thousands and condemn me in the process... What is everyone else capable of?

What am *I* capable of?

Shuddering, I gulp back my fear and close my eyes. Blowing out a breath, I try to calm myself, try to tell myself that I don't need to find a bar before we leave Termana.

Just get through this, and you'll be back on Sparrow, back in the stars.

When I finish recounting Lachlan's attack and the information he leaked to my mother, leading to the attack on Odyssey, Croon and Martine turn to Lachlan, requesting a defense.

He sits there, silent and broken. He musters only a shake of his head.

His counselor, a middle-aged man with pale brown skin, asks for a lessened sentence due to temporary insanity, a truly desperate plea.

Chemical castration can't be much better than death, after all, and one way or another, they won't let him go on to procreate.

"Temporary insanity may be the case," Judge Martine says. "But his conduct surpassed anything that can be forgiven by temporary insanity. Not only did he attempt to take a life himself, but his actions directly lead to the deaths of thousands of Regonians and several of our own citizens."

My breath hitches, and my heart stutters.

Because I know what comes next.

"There's only one sentence I can hand down," Judge Martine says. "The penalty is death, to be carried out this evening. Lachlan, you'll have the rest of the afternoon to say your goodbyes, if you wish."

He sits there, unmoving.

But tears pour over my cheeks.

***

"Scrape by Chelsea Wolfe. 2017." hisses from the speakers with distorted instruments. Eerie humming and high feminine vocals follow. Breathy words crash upon my ears as I cradle the bottle against my chest, leaning back in my chair. Dark brown poison sloshes in the glass bottle, just enough left to send me into a peaceful, dreamless slumber.

Thank god for the good stuff.

I tip the bottle back, draining more of the Perrin whiskey, savoring the burn of it. The homebrew stuff would fell most grown men, but with my tolerance, it should be just enough.

I stare at my laptop, resting in my chair across the room, and disbelief swirls through me on listless waves.

Atlantis is done.

Years of work, so much time and effort, and it's finally done.

But guilt freezes my veins.

Too late.

My defense program is done and already hard at work, guarding us from further interference and abductions, installed in the net, working its way through the entirety of our world. The Drennar will get nothing from us now, but the Regonians still suffer.

Two thousand souls… gone.

I take another drink, closing my eyes to block it all out, but the sight of their shaking bodies flickers through my mind.

They're gone.

And for what?

We may have lost ten times that many to the Drennar, but that isn't a good enough reason.

My dad appears in my mind, staring at me as I watched a Drennar steal him away from our home in my place. I fall back, leaning against the bed. The rough edge of the frame digs into my back, but I don't move.

"I'm sorry, Dad," I whisper, words starting to slur. "I should've finished it sooner."

Guilt fills my mind, hazy and terrible, obscuring everything. A tear pricks at one eye, and I blink it away.

I take another drink. Struggling to line the cap up with the bottle, missing a few times, I close it and set it aside with a thunk. My head lolls on my shoulders, and I can feel sleep coming for me, feel it reaching, tugging at my eyelids.

The door opens, and the light from the hall pierces my eyes as Ricardo comes in for the night. He looks at the bottle, looks me over. A deep sigh lifts his shoulders.

"I'll be sober by the time we need to leave. Don't worry." Petulance tinges my words, but so does the alcohol, dragging them out, running them together.

"You're better than this, Olivia," Ricardo says. He shakes his head, walking toward the bathroom as the door to the hall shuts.

"How would you know?" I challenge.

He barely knows me. He doesn't know the idiot, the irresponsible fuck up, that lurks beneath the surface.

But he's seeing me now.

I reach for the bottle, toss the lid aside, and take another drink.

He pauses in the doorway to the bathroom, turning to look back at me. "Because I know the types of people who fall to the bottle. I know the types of people who *deserve* to drown in it." The expression on his face softens as he searches my features. "That isn't you."

He steps into the bathroom, leaving me alone with my thoughts, alone with my guilt. My stomach flops.

Unsteady hands lift dark brown glass to my lips, and I try not to let the color remind me of my mother's eyes as I take another long drink. My throat burns, but I savor the feeling, savor the relief it promises.

I sigh contentedly as the shelves and tapestries slant and fracture into doubles. I close my eyes to stave off the dizziness, but I know how this goes, know that relief is just moments away.

My Link glows bright, and a harsh, shrill sound replaces my music.

My alarm.

I silence it, let the song finish. With one more swig from the bottle, I cap it and set it aside. But the cap doesn't quite seat properly, and I knock it over.

A few precious droplets spill onto the floor, soak into the blankets laid out there.

I hurry to set it right, but the cap is too much of a challenge. Blinking slowly, I stand the bottle upright and give up.

Time for sleep.

I yearn for more, but I have to fly everyone to Termana for my mother's tribunal in the morning. I have to be sober by then.

My eyes flutter as I roll onto my hands and knees, wondering when I fell over to begin with. I push myself up, crawling into bed, tilting my head as the room slants.

But it only tips further.

A tiny voice in the back of my head whispers that it's all my fault, but the alcohol quiets it, puts a finger to its lips and tells it to hush.

My limbs fight me, refusing to do my bidding as I pull myself into bed. Collapsing half on the mattress, I close my eyes and dream of nothing.

Just the way I like it.

Chapter Six
Novay

Reginald

Sitting next to Rone on my bed, I pop a water orb into my mouth. My hands tremble from the day's tests. After two days of grading me in math and science, they finally showed me the rest of that night.

I watched Eva threaten our daughter, watched her tell living, breathing, sentient people that they were disposable.

I watched her pull the trigger and kill two thousand people without batting an eye.

The sight of them, convulsing in their beds as electricity surged through them, defenseless in unconsciousness, flickers through my mind, over and over.

But I can't bear to think of it any longer. I can't change it. It happened nearly two weeks ago on another planet. Sent just a couple days ago, my message to Olivia may not have even reached her, yet.

There's nothing I can do.

So, I ask, "Why are they testing my emotions? Why now, after 12 years? And why did they make you get that experiment done? Don't get me wrong, I'm glad you have emotions, now, but… why?"

Rone looks at me, smiling shyly as she tips her head to the side. "I proposed the experiment, then volunteered to be the prototype. I just… didn't realize it would change me so much."

She reaches out, taking my hand easily. My heart races. Her gaze falls to our hands as her thumb moves slowly over my skin.

"We've studied Humans for years, measuring your race in all quantifiable ways. All the ways we assumed were important. We never questioned that you would make decisions the way we do. We minimized the impact of emotion at every turn. But intellect isn't the driving force of humanity. Emotion is."

A short laugh bursts from me, drawing her attention to my face. But she goes on.

"We know nothing about Humans because we don't understand emotion, something so strong as to touch every aspect of your life, sometimes even jeopardizing the entire human race as it plunged your whole world into war." Her shoulders lift with a sigh. "Emotions are so much more than we ever thought. They change everything."

I swallow back a lump in my throat. The electric blue striations move across her green irises, shifting as she lines up some piece of a puzzle greater than my comprehension.

My eyes dip to her lips, but only briefly.

"Are there…" I clear my throat, then start again. "Are there no other species out there that have emotions? We can't be the only ones. Krona and Tenna, wherever they're from, they clearly have emotions."

"That they do…" she mumbles, dropping her gaze. Her face falls into a frown. "Krona and Tenna are members of Daen Tribe, a part of the Flori cluster on Regonia One. Taron Tribe, Roon Tribe, and the Vaerkin make up the rest of the Flori cluster, and they are all part of an anomaly. Only one other cluster on Regonia One, Two, or Three developed that way. We thought, for a long time, that they regressed, evolutionarily speaking. Now, I'm not so sure."

She leans against me, letting her head fall to my shoulder. Soft heat radiates through me, melting some of the numbness from my bones. I wrap one arm around her, letting it land on the small of her back, carefully below her wings.

*How I've missed being close to someone, feeling...
maybe not loved but... wanted? Appreciated?*

I lean my head forward, peering at Rone's soft grey features. A tear slides over her cheek, and I tip her head up with my forefinger.

"What is it?" I ask.

She slowly shakes her head, and her eyes waver before mine. "All these experiments..." she mumbles, but her voice trails off.

Does she feel... guilty?

"Would it help to talk about it?" I offer.

Not because it might grant me information about the Drennar. Not because I hope to use her to find a way home. But because I don't want to see her cry. Because I want to see her happy.

I want to help her feel better.

"I can't." Her eyes falter before mine, landing on her lap.

"You could," I say. "It's not like I can tell anyone about it."

A morbid chuckle escapes my lips, and a hopeless one leaves her.

Reaching up, she places a hand on the side of my face, pulling me close. But she doesn't kiss me. She leans her forehead against mine.

"Yours is not the only experiment I was assigned to," she begins, but a sob chokes her words. "There is another planet, Gordeky. Many of us monitor its progression. The people there were born of us, but all variation in appearance, all pigment, was stripped away to eliminate differences that have caused tension on other worlds. Even their temperaments were adjusted, made docile. All except for two. We wished to study the effects of one violent, angry being and one hopeful one on an otherwise stagnant society."

Touching the side of her head, still clean-shaven since gaining emotion, Rone says, "Before, their plight was a curious thing, another anomaly. But now…" Her face scrunches, and a sob punctuates her confession. "Now, I see how they suffer, and I hate what we've done."

"There's a device on the sister planet, Meruna, that could reprogram the violent one, but most are so docile, so timid, they dare not hope it more than a legend. And this morning, before I came to see you, I watched the latest descendant of the hopeful line…" Rone tips her head back, letting the tears slide down her temples. "She's only a child, and the attack was so vicious. I'm not sure she'll survive."

My heart aches at the thought of an entire society suffering, at the thought of a child lying half dead on some faraway planet, and at the suffering of the woman before me.

Rone pulls away, wiping her eyes. "You must hate me. I'm no better than Eva."

"You are, though."

She jerks her head toward me, staring into my eyes with her brows furrowed in confusion.

So, I explain, "You didn't know, but she did. You feel remorse, and she doesn't."

Even though your world should have kept you from remorse and compassion, even though our world should have carved it into Eva's bones.

A fresh bout of tears pours over Rone's cheeks, and I pull her against me. She nestles into my embrace, soft lips brushing the sensitive skin of my neck.

I pull in a deep, shuddering breath.

Chapter Seven
Novay

Rone

Sitting in Reginald's quarters, I summon old documentaries of humanity, speeding through them in my mind. Several times, they descended into all-out war, jeopardizing the entire race. I skip over most of it, scanning for a few specific sections of Human history.

I watch Nazis mercilessly experiment on prisoners in internment camps. I watch Prime Minister Valsen take an entire country hostage with the express intention of experimenting on those poor captured souls, spurring the third world war.

I pull up videos of Eva's various experiments, watch her authorize many heinous acts, actively participating in most.

And we're no better.

I'm *no better.*

Reginald's words whisper through my mind. "You didn't know, but she did. You feel remorse, and she doesn't." The tone of his voice, so compassionate, so understanding…

Could he be right?

Is that all it takes to be better?

I review the footage again, watching the Humans' faces, listening to the tone of their voices. I try, desperately, to suss out their emotions, relying on a thing the Humans call intuition, a thing I used to think was nonsense.

And somehow, I hear anger in their tones, simmering underneath their words. I see the tensing of their hands, feel the disappointment in their gazes as they stare at unresponsive subjects or failed experiments, and though I've watched it before, I see the gestures for the involuntary emotional responses they are.

But never do I see or hear remorse. I never glimpse a hint of sadness or sympathy.

Is Reginald right?

My heart leaps at the prospect of being better than these people, being better than Eva. I shrug off all the possible implications of why I might wish to be better than her specifically, ignoring the little spike in my heart rate at being tolerable to Reginald.

But is remorse truly enough?

My mind whips through data, comparing the actions of those tormentors with the actions of my people, with my own actions. But my heart is already making plans.

Impossible plans.

No, not impossible.

Already, I see the ways it could work, the steps necessary to *make* it work, to make things better.

For Reginald. For Olivia.

For all our subjects.

But can I do it?

A long sigh escapes me. Reginald still holds me in his arms, and I tighten my own embrace.

Then, I take the first step, submitting all my data. Everything I've been holding onto, all my emotions and illogical thoughts sync with the Drennar network, and my ears blink three times. I shudder at the sudden illumination of the room, hating that it's so obvious, hating that Reginald might think I'm submitting something about him.

I could tell him that someone sent me a transmission. But he doesn't ask, and my nerves hold my tongue still.

My heart flutters in my chest, and my stomach ties itself in knots. But the expected response comes with three more flashes from my ears.

They don't understand what I've sent out. More data is necessary to draw any reliable conclusions.

My rank drops 1.4% for withholding data rather than syncing immediately, and my stomach drops.

Does my ranking even matter?

I never would've been allowed to breed anyway.

A lance of pain shoots through me, sudden and unexpected. The human idea of motherhood paints itself across my mind, and longing sweeps through me.

But it never would have been like that, even if my ranking were high enough.

Chapter Eight
Odyssey Space Research Station

Tenna

Hot water runs over my body. I wash slowly, mind full of the coming tribunal. The door to the bathroom hangs open, and I hear a hollow thunk as the bass' body hits the side of its case. For a moment, I wonder if he'll try to play it, but no sound greets my ears.

Sighing at the lack of music, I decide to play my own, supplying the Link with my thoughts. From the speaker in the bedroom "100 years by Serj Tankian. 2016." starts to play.

The gentle instruments ease my nerves, though only just. My mind buzzes with the difficulties I know we'll face at the tribunal. Even if the Survival Coalition agrees to our demands, we'll be hard pressed to keep our people from taking their revenge.

They're angry. And rightly so.

I picture my brother, wondering where they might have him stashed, and my hands curl into tight fists in my hair.

Steam billows through the bathroom, but it seems to have a scent. Blinking, I wipe a hand over my face.

Am I losing my mind? Steam has no scent.

But this is no steam.

A memory slams into me with all the force of a physical blow, and suddenly, the steam around me smells a lot like Bellona flowers.

And the descent of man overcomes me.

In my mind, I run through our village as five strange metal ships hover overhead, visitors from the Realm of Stars. Screams of fear ring out all around me, piercing my eardrums. A few of my people stand between their houses, staring up at the ships with awe on their faces.

"They've come back!" one shouts. "The Drennar have returned for us!"

But these are not the ships from our history. These great hulking things look nothing like the sleek, blue-grey ships of our ancestors.

And if there is anything to be learned from the fate of the Drennar, it's that we can expect nothing good to come from the stars.

I shout for my people to run, to take shelter in their homes. I call out for our warriors to prepare themselves.

Krona reaches my side, huffing from his sprint from the Vyrto fields. Our armor lies in the keep, too far to do us any good, but warriors flock to our sides.

Ports open on the sides of the ships, and gas billows outward. It settles over the village like a fog, drifting in lazy clouds. The unmistakable sweet scent of Bellona flowers pervades every synapse, and I know we won't have much time to defend our people.

"Take shelter!" I shout. "Close your homes to the gas!"

Heart pounding, I push a few people into stone cottages, wrenching the doors shut behind them. Krona and our warriors do the same.

But more gas spills into the air.

Coughing on it, I grow dizzy.

NO!

Shaking my head to clear it, I watch the first ship descend. It settles onto the ground, eerily silent. With a series of whirs and clicks, a panel opens, lowering itself to the ground like a ramp.

Tiny beings pour out like insects. Clad in black from head to toe, they move jerkily.

How much does their armor weigh?

They lift strange cylinders before themselves, pointing them at us. Rage fills me, for I know they mean us harm. I feel it in my bones, in my gut.

My head spins with the Bellona gas. My body protests every movement, suddenly weak and tired. A few warriors collapse behind me.

"SVE!" I shout. *Battle!*

And we charge.

The first projectile slams into me, and one of their little black cylinders kicks up. But the projectile doesn't break my skin.

Their weapons are weak.

A drowsy smile lifts the corners of my lips. We run, slamming into the puny soldiers. Bones snap in a frail body as I collide with the one whose projectile hit me. He goes down silently.

But I fall beside him, off balance.

The world spins beneath me as I try to stand, choking on the gas that still pours from their ships. I topple over once more, hands grasping for purchase and finding it in the bulky armor of these strange beasts. The creature falls with me, and I drag it closer. Muscle memory guides me, and I snap the frail being's neck.

Pushing myself to my knees, stomach swirling with nausea, I wonder how much Bellona this is. I've never taken so much as to have ill effects. The tiny flowers always seemed so harmless, never causing so much as a headache.

Looking up, I see Krona stumble toward me. He falls, reaching out a hand. Dragging myself closer, I twine my fingers with his, then collapse beside him.

His eyelids flutter, then fall shut.

I glance out at the first battlefield I wasn't prepared for. Efsi, my brother, charges at one of the star-born creatures. His face contorts with rage, but his steps are sluggish as he weaves toward an alien soldier.

The creature of the stars points one of those strange cylinders at Efsi, and the device bucks. This time, the projectile finds its mark, sinking into one of Efsi's turquoise eyes.

Blood pours out, flowing over ash-colored skin.

My heart shatters, and he drops to his knees. Time slows, splintering, burning this moment into me. Efsi falls back, blood gushing freely to pool about his head, to mat his white hair into clumps.

A scream wrenches itself free of my throat.

I push myself to hands and knees, and rage curls my fingers into claws, digging my nails into the dirt. Snarling, I try to steady myself so I can strangle the creature that killed my brother.

The stupid beast approaches me.

Grabbing them by the ankle, I jerk them down. I rip their pitiful excuse for a helmet off in one fell swoop, casting it aside. Staring down at the creature beneath me, I scream, voice breaking as fury rips through my throat.

Fear shines in peculiar brown eyes, but a small canister appears before my face. A cloud of gas erupts, choking me. I cough and splutter, but I rip the canister from glove-clad hands, then smash it down into that strange, tan face.

As I fall to my side, I hiss at the fallen soldier, "Oal hoo mai kai taeark." *May your sound never be found.*

Rolling to my side, I take Krona's hand in mine. His chest rises and falls steadily, but I don't hear his breath. All I hear are the too-heavy footsteps of small, cowardly beasts claiming my village and the whirring and clicking of another ship's ramp lowering to the ground.

Then, darkness claims me.

And I come back to myself.

In the shower, Krona kneels before me, shaking my shoulders. Curled into a ball on the floor, I look up at him. Water pelts my skin, suddenly far too warm for my liking. My scalp prickles, and my stomach roils. A deep rage shakes me to my core, searing every fiber of my being.

"What's wrong?" Krona asks, voice urgent and pleading. "Are you okay?"

"I remember," I say, voice a sharp hiss. "I remember the day they came for us."

***

Krona and I lead our people onto a massive ship docked outside the station rather than inside the hangar with the smaller crafts. Tension and anxiety swirl in the air around our Tribe. Tempers flare, and my nerves begin to fray.

Just over four thousand souls pass by us, some stomping so hard the ramp dents and others dragging their feet, eyes downcast. I trace the lines of their faces, the slump of their shoulders.

And my own heart fractures just a little bit more as I take in the empty spaces they leave for the loved ones lost in the attack. A man stops, looking over his shoulder, only to deflate as whoever he searches for doesn't turn up. A woman reaches out, hand plumbing the depths of empty air for a hand she often holds.

A hand she *held*.

Tears slip over grey skin of every shade. I steady myself, letting my own tears fall, but standing straight. Those who meet my gaze nod, and their eyes shine with the same need for justice that burns in my chest.

But as they all cram into the cargo hold, tempers rise. Someone shouts. Another drives a fist into a piece of equipment sitting in the middle of the room, cracking its outer shell.

The blood drains from me, because this isn't what we need. The Humans here are helping us, taking us where we need to go. Fear slithers through my veins, icy and sharp, at the thought that Olivia or Ricardo or Dr. Sullivan might come to harm if our people fall to their rage in such a confined space.

I tug on Krona's hand, then sprint into the cargo hold. I launch myself upward, grabbing the catwalk above us and hauling myself up. Krona follows quickly, and we address our people, calling for their attention.

But only those nearest us hear, turning to face us, to wait for our words.

Krona's parents climb up onto another catwalk, sprinting to join us, calling for attention as they come.

And then I see my sister, Kala, separate from the crowd as she leaps up to grab the catwalk. The sea of faces below recognize her, see her dark figure and hear her shouts for order.

My knees weaken, and I clutch the railing so hard it crinkles like foil.

She's alive...

Melnara, my sister's partner, climbs up after her, white hair loose about her shoulders as she directs attention our way.

And finally, my parents climb up. Krona steadies me when I stumble.

But with their Inerans and our families demanding attention, our people settle down.

I'll go to them soon. My people need me, now.

"I know the tragedies we've suffered are great. I know the losses we all feel," I say.

My people search the catwalk, finding the holes this nightmare has left within my family. My own eyes search for Efsi, half expecting him to climb up onto a catwalk.

But he doesn't surface.

And neither does his partner, Rimahn.

Did she die on Regonia or here?

Taking a deep breath, I say, "We will demand our justice soon. But we must maintain our composure. The Humans responsible for this are not present, and those that are here are allies. We cannot destroy the objects of their aid, cannot jeopardize the safety of people who are friends to our cause."

Heads nod below us, while others fall, ashamed of their own behavior.

"These are trying times, I know," I say, voice falling so low that if anyone else made a sound, I'm not sure they'd hear me.

But the cargo hold is silent, save my words.

Krona takes my hand, showing our people our unity, our strength.

"Draw strength from each other," I say. "Cherish those you still have, for soon, we demand justice for those we lost."

Our people cry out, but this time in approval and righteousness rather than fury. Slowly, they settle in, and I don't move until I'm sure they'll be still, be safe.

Then I sprint down the catwalk, pulling Krona along with me, and fall into my parents' arms. My heart splinters, and tears spill forth.

Kala and Melnara approach, wrapping their arms around us all, and again, I find myself waiting, expecting Efsi and Rimahn to join us.

A sob breaks through me when they don't.

***

Olivia's spacecraft ferries us out into the vast blackness of the Realm of Stars. Krona and I meander to the bridge, stopping just outside the cockpit to gaze through the glass of a viewport.

A disorienting mixture of awe and emptiness fills me, and I turn from it, glancing instead at Krona. He stands beside me, too tall to fit in one of the seats clearly only meant for Humans.

"Hoo kai voo mai," I whisper. *You are my sound.*

"Hoo kai voo mai," he answers.

I squeeze his hand, glad to have him here with me. My time on Odyssey without him felt so empty, even if I didn't realize the cause at the time, what with my memory gone. But even now, a chill runs down my spine, and I shudder at the thought of losing him.

Looking back out the window, I stare at Termana. The massive metal ball seems like it should fall, but there's nothing beneath it, nothing around it.

Nothing to ground it.

Another thing I never considered about the expanse beyond our world.

A strange tube sticking out of the metal ball, an airlock, opens. Given what Olivia said about space, I expect a whooshing sound, some sucking feeling, but nothing flies in or out. No errant objects impact our ship, and nothing waits inside.

My stomach flutters, but I remind myself that we aren't leading our people into a hotbed of hostile aliens.

Olivia broadcast the whole thing, let everyone know what was going on.

And from the chatter on the net, most of the people on Termana seem like they won't mind what Krona and I intend to propose.

Blowing out a breath, I steady myself as the ship descends through the opening into a barren metal box. A jolt rocks through the ship, but my bent knees absorb the mild impact as Olivia sets the ship down.

Great vents open outside, pumping gas in, and for a moment, I fear it might be the Bellona gas again. But Olivia doesn't flinch, just turns knobs and dials, flipping switches with only compulsory glances at the control panels before her.

She moves deftly even as she grimaces at the bright lights that flicker on outside the ship. Ricardo's lips purse, just barely, almost imperceptibly, and he shakes his head.

I study Olivia, and this time, I see the dark circles under her eyes, the lines that have etched themselves into her forehead in the past days. Something beeps loudly, and she winces.

Is she…

What did they call it? Hungover?

I tip my head to the side, wondering why she drinks so heavily if this is the consequence.

90

But then I look at Ricardo, puzzled by the sadness lingering in his gaze as he watches her, and I let my mind indulge in this idle curiosity, giving myself a break from the pressing matters of the tribunal.

What hurdle have they thrown in the way of the feelings they clearly hold for each other?

But even that line of thinking can only distract me for a moment before the coming events weigh upon me once more. The fate of our people hangs on the outcome of this tribunal, just as it seems to have balanced so precariously on every single breath these past few days.

Every choice, every word, make or break.

For if our demands find the Humans unwilling to cooperate, not only will the alliance necessary to shirk the hold of the Drennar collapse before we can even build it, but we'll have no way home.

Though, maybe even those that find our terms unsavory will see the logic of not further angering a clearly superior race of warriors.

I really hope I don't have to use force against them.

But for our people…

In the cockpit, Olivia, Ricardo, and Dr. Sullivan unbuckle and rise to their full heights, coming up almost to our shoulders. A moment of surprise registers in Dr. Sullivan's eyes, even after so long in our company, as he looks at us, then tips his head back to meet my gaze.

If it still catches him off guard, someone reasonably comfortable with us, what will the Humans on Termana think?

Sighing, I turn to lead Krona back to the cargo bay.

Time to find out.

Chapter Nine
Termana

Olivia

I trudge through the shell that surrounds Termana with just over 4,000 Regonians following in my wake. I let my Link fill my head with music, trying desperately to drown out the maelstrom of guilt. "Since We've Been Wrong by The Mars Volta. 2009." whispers through me, riding on waves of gentle guitar and vocals.

I drag myself forward, eyes drifting over the utilitarian halls, so sparse and lifeless. I lift my gaze to the ceiling, the thick metal hull separating us from space and a quick, cold death.

I could always go into an airlock and open the door.

I close my eyes, gritting my teeth against the guilt that washes through me over everything that's happened. Turning my gaze forward, I hug my arms tightly around myself, careful not to look anyone in the eyes lest they see it written across my face.

Tenna, Krona, and Ricardo, especially.

The rest of the Regonians might not see it, too disoriented by this place and everything they've learned, everything they've lost, since yesterday.

My brows reach for each other.

Has it really only been a day since we woke them?

I look back at the Regonians, carefully avoiding my friends. A few people shiver. With rage or confusion? With the cold of the hangar and the shell?

Turning forward once more, I turn the volume up higher within my mind, grateful that my only task is to walk.

Surely even a fuck-up like me can manage that much.

Wandering through the outer shell, I lead the people past service ladders and toward the bank of freight elevators. With a few simple commands, I open them all at once, and the Regonians split into their assigned groups. Some follow Tenna into an elevator, some go with Krona. Ricardo takes a group, as do each of Tenna's and Krona's family members.

Well, their surviving family members, anyway.

Tenna's brother and his partner cloud my mind, and I turn my music up louder. I try to distract myself as my group files into the elevator, wondering if the Regonians get motion sick.

Will the cleaning crews have to hose these things out?

After all, even with our warnings, these move faster than the one on Odyssey.

I step in with my group, tucking into the 20 meter by 20 meter elevator with a couple hundred enormous warriors. They tower over me, squash in next to me, crowding on all sides. The doors close, and the air grows heavy, pressing down on me, weighed down by their anxiety.

I close my eyes, turn my music up louder, until I hear nothing beyond me. Bracing myself, I send a quick message to the leaders of the other groups, warn my own group, then signal the elevators to descend.

My stomach leaps into my throat as we drop, nearly free-falling, and I clench my hands into fists. The brakes engage, slowing us at a startling rate, and I take a step forward, steadying myself, as we settle.

Swallowing, I open the elevators and tumble out. People spill out around me, gathering together. The air shifts as

98

they reunite, and tears fill their eyes, even after such a short separation.

Have I ever cared so much for someone?

My dad's face pops into my mind, staring at me over the shoulder of a Drennar soldier.

He gave himself up for me.

And this... 2,000 dead, twice that many stranded away from their home... This is how I repay him?

I shove the image of him away, unable to support its weight today. The music blares in my mind, but I need it louder, need to push the thoughts far away, somewhere I can forget about them.

My hands clench, and I wish for a tumbler of Perrin. The signs of a budding addiction swirl through my mind, red flags flapping in a wind of guilt. But I shove that away too.

Because really, what's the point in fighting it?

Atlantis is done. Too late, but it's done.

What else is there for me to do?

With Daen Tribe reunited and the rest of our little trek lingering beyond the freight doors, I cut my music short. The sudden silence in my mind screams louder than the music did.

All of Daen Tribe stands before me, uncertain, scared, angry. Clenched fists and tear-filled eyes watch me, needing someone confident and comforting to guide them.

But all they have is me.

I swallow, staring at them, at the varied shades of grey in their skin, the full spectrum of blue showcased in their hair. I look up at them, short even next to most of their children.

My knees wobble at the sight of them, this alien army, these alien people.

Their eyes, a million shades of emerald and jade and mint, shine with fear and humanity and love.

And loss.

How could Mommy Dearest have looked at them like lab rats?

They might be more human than we are.

But then, what I learned of her experiments on Bolivia Station, right before the Drennar's slaughter, doesn't bode well for what she was willing to do to humans either.

And something clicks into place.

The reason Mother wasn't punished for what happened on Bolivia Station.

I turned it all in to Robert Mulvaney, surreptitiously planting the files on his Link, in plain view, so a tribunal could be held and mother could be stopped.

But Mother got off scot-free, and the only one sought out was the hacker who got into official files.

Because he was in on it, even then.

Sighing, I nod, thankful I was careful enough not to leave a trace of myself in his Link, not to risk it.

Then, a sick feeling grows within me, a fear of something worse. Maybe paranoia, maybe just an educated guess, given what they did on Odyssey Station.

I vow to look up footage of the Bolivia Station slaughter before the tribunal starts, steeling myself for what I might find.

Because if my gut is right, there might be more crimes to be paid for.

Chapter Ten
Termana

Krona

I slip my hand into Tenna's, and we lead our people down a hard road, trudging to the auditorium modified to fit us all for the tribunal. Crowds of Humans stare at us as we pass, shouting questions from behind guard rails, held back by soldiers.

It all washes over me, unreal and unbelievable. At any moment, I expect to wake, cozy in my bed on Regonia, only to turn to Tenna and speak faster than the wind, trying to tell her of my fantastical and terrifying dreams.

But I've never been a man of creativity.

Facts and deduction, emotion and intuition. Those are the realms I walk.

Not pure creation.

To populate the stars with people with amber eyes and red hair, people who destroyed their own world then made a new one?

I glance up at the strange metal shell of this place, barely visible beyond the blinding lights that shine down from it, and know I'd never dream of such a thing. With a glance at my Tribe, at eyes painted a million shades of sorrow and loss and thirst for vengeance, I see the same incredulity reflected back at me.

I pull open the door on the large, square metal building, wishing I could tell them that yes, this is a dream. We'll all wake up soon.

If only it were that simple.

We file into the tiny auditorium, cram ourselves into chairs that squeeze our hips. Tenna, Olivia, Doctor Sullivan, and I take our seats at the front of our people, facing a round stage in the center of a room that's massive by Human standards.

And we wait.

I survey the place, getting my bearings, wondering what kinds of technology might exist within these seemingly plain walls. Unable to guess at the things hidden away from me, I refocus my attention on what matters.

Justice. An alliance. Answers.

A way home.

Humans file in, filling the other half of the auditorium. They gawk at us, not-quite-whispering, filling the entire place with the noise of a waever infestation. My mind fills with the pesky feathered beasts, blending in with our grem crops, looking so much like the ripe purple fruits that an entire field might be devoured before we noticed them if not for the insufferable noise of the creatures.

But our people stare too, lending a lower-pitched susurration to the cacophony as they marvel at the tiny Humans and the world they built among the stars.

A small door at the back of the stage opens, and the room stills. Led and flanked by Soldiers, the Coalition enters with two judges in tow. They all glance at us, apologies written clearly across their faces, as they shuffle to sit near a podium at center stage.

And then, the main doors are thrown wide. Thousands of heads turn as we all stare.

Eva Dobovich, Robert Mulvaney, and all their co-conspirators shuffle through the doors with their hands bound. Armed soldiers escort them to seats near the stage.

Tension fills the auditorium, and rage boils the air. An icy cloud of fear seems to hang over the perpetrators. My eyes dance over them, tallying them up.

Roughly 500.

A disappointingly high number.

On stage, Johnathan Croon, Minister of Human Affairs, stands and approaches the podium. His sleek navy-blue suit lends him a polished air, far more so than the pajamas of last night. His silver hair is slicked back, and his eyes sparkle with nervous energy. The crinkles that edge them turn his look of distinction to one of mournful regret.

Screens light up overhead, showing his image, and speakers throughout the auditorium magnify his voice. I hope we've prepared our people enough for this as he says, "Good people of Termana, Daen Tribe of Regonia, I wish with all my heart that we could have met under better circumstances. Thus far, our species' introductions to alien life forms have been nothing short of disastrous."

He glances down at the podium, running a hand over his face.

"First and foremost," he begins, lifting his gaze as his practiced air falls away. "I'd like to apologize. On behalf, not only of the Survival Coalition, but of the entire Human race. We're sorry. *I'm* sorry. This *never* should've happened. Daen Tribe should not have been forcibly involved in our war. You should *not* have been kidnapped. You shouldn't have been used as lab rats or attacked."

Again, he pauses, but only briefly, eyes searching the faces of our people.

"Your friends, your family …" His voice breaks, but he clears his throat to continue. "They shouldn't have been killed."

My eyes prick with tears as I picture Efsi's smile, remember the way he and Tenna used to laugh together.

Behind Croon, the rest of the innocent Coalition members stand and approach him. All but one raise their right hands, the remainder, a pudgy man in a too-neat suit, raises his left.

I stare at them, wondering what strange Human tradition this might be.

Then, as one, they say, "We solemnly swear to do everything in our power to see justice done this day and to uphold the safety and survival of the Human race."

As they return to their seats, Croon sighs, then continues.

"There is more than enough evidence to convict all involved. As such, an overwhelming amount of guilty pleas, all framed with self-justification and made with the hopes of lessening sentences, have poured in, allowing us to entirely skip the conviction portion of this tribunal."

He glances back at the rest of the Coalition members, clearly uncomfortable, then turns forward, and I wonder if this type of thing would typically fall to that vile creature, Mulvaney.

Croon reads a few official sounding statements, then hands the podium off to one of the judges on stage, introducing her as, "The Honorable Judge Supreme Akira Lucille Martine, the highest authority of the Defense department who wasn't party to these terrible proceedings."

Clad in a black robe with a white collar, her graying hair pinned back in a tight bun, she steps up to the podium. Her clear brown eyes scan the room, shrewd and intelligent. Disgust colors them when she takes in the crowd of offenders, and her lips purse.

Then, the tortuously boring tribunal truly commences.

Five hundred and six times, she calls a name and asks if they stand by their statements. Five hundred and six times, the answer is yes.

The fools believe in what they did.

My stomach churns in a mixture of disgust and rage. But maybe they have another motive, given Olivia's descriptions of these tribunals. Maybe they aren't dumb enough to think forcing the Coalition into showing footage of their deeds to everyone here would help them. Even if a few tried to claim they were following orders, they'd surely only reveal their willingness later in their statements.

I blow out a breath, heart burning with a hatred stronger than I've ever known. My fists clench the metal armrests of my chair, and they crumple in my grip.

Beside me, Tenna's knuckles whiten similarly, and she draws in a breath. Her eyes burn, staring daggers at any Human who speaks of the supposed *underlying ethics* of their actions.

Hours of this madness drag on until Judge Martine finally reaches Mulvaney and Dobovich. "Do you stand by your statements?" she asks Mulvaney.

"Of course, I do," he spits. "And as the only person actually qualified to handle this, I demand that these proceedings be stopped. We have work to do, and you're wasting our time."

He's right about that much. This is a colossal waste.

"Even now, you feel yourself justified to say such things?" Judge Martine asks. "As per clause 5.2 of the Treaty of the Founding of the Survival Coalition, you have been stripped of all authority."

I seethe, waiting for this to end, for justice to come.

"You are no longer eligible to dictate orders, and you've never been eligible for lenience. As a member of the Coalition, you were held to a higher standard. You swore oaths to uphold the laws of our people and to serve that which is *good and right* while maintaining our survival. You betrayed your oaths, thereby relieving yourself of any power your position may have once afforded you."

I sit up straighter, chin lifting.

Judge Martine goes on, voice grave, "The gravity of your position as Minister will now grant you a stricter punishment, as you broke a great deal more laws, promises, oaths, and responsibilities than anyone else here, save Miss Dobovich, of course."

At least they mean to hold their leaders to higher standards.

"You DARE take that tone with me?!" Mulvaney screams, surging forward, finally at his limit.

Soldiers descend on him, dragging him back before he manages even two steps.

"I *put* you in those robes!" Mulvaney shouts, face red. "You wouldn't *be* here if it weren't for me, you sniveling, old crone!"

Our people stir, aching to snap this man in half, and the air shifts. The creak of the chairs, the swish of their clothes, and the shuffle of boots on the floor fill the room. Hisses of fury passing through their lips draw nervous glances from the Humans across the auditorium.

But Mulvaney rages on.

He rants, straining against the soldiers who hold him, spitting fury at this woman who's only trying to do what's right. I grit my teeth, clench my jaw.

But I force myself to unfurl my fists, releasing what's left of my armrests.

For our people, I have to compose myself, if only to show them that it's possible.

Mulvaney slams his forehead against one of the soldier's noses, and blood gushes out. The man doesn't flinch. With a single blow, he knocks the former Minister of Defense unconscious. The other soldiers catch Mulvaney, lowering him back into his chair.

The entire auditorium sags with relief, and satisfaction rushes through me as I watch Mulvaney's head loll.

One of the soldiers whips out a small bottle, and I furrow my brows. I tense, half expecting the scent of Bellona, but when they spritz it in front of Mulvaney's face, a tangy scent drifts toward us. Mulvaney jolts awake, jilted into consciousness by some strange Human chemical.

Martine purses her lips. "That's regrettable."

Then she turns to Eva Dobovich. The former Minister rises to her feet, chin held aloft. She casts a disappointed glance at her counterpart, one brow raised and jaw clenched, but I can't tell if self-control or cold-heartedness keeps her acidic eyes from boiling over.

"Eva Dobovich," Judge Supreme Martine addresses her, stripping her of her title. "Do you stand by the statement you gave and your admission of guilt in these matters?"

Eva doesn't bat an eye.

"I do," she says. "We are no longer the biggest threat to our survival, and we must address the real threat appropriately, even if that means sacrifice. We sacrificed when it came time to leave Earth. We left so many behind. We've sacrificed repeatedly since then."

She stands up taller, but I can't fathom the choice to leave an entire planet full of people to die. My chest expands with a deep breath as I try to calm myself.

"We've all done things we didn't want to because we had to," Dobovich goes on. "We treated every problem with the severity it deserved, as I have been doing with the threat of the Drennar. We are still the *Survival* Coalition, whether anyone remembers that in their day-to-day life or not."

Martine's brow raises. "This is true. We deal with every problem with the severity it deserves," she says. "And now, we must deal with you, with all the severity *you* deserve."

Martine's Link flashes bright red in perfect unison with those of the other Coalition members. They all stare down at the devices buried in their wrists, and I lean forward, heart leaping into my throat.

What could be so important as to distract them now?

Horror flashes over Martine's face, over all their faces, as they watch their Links. Martine shakes her head back and forth. She swallows, eyes landing on Olivia when she looks up.

I turn to my Human friend, really looking at her for the first time today. Her colorful eyes are dull, and the light has left her lustrous skin, leaving it the color of dry dirt rather than the rich, warm brown it normally tends toward. Even her hair no longer shines.

What broke her?

She's held on through so much, but what could have possibly broken her?

The emptiness in her eyes frightens me, for her sake and for ours.

Whatever has finally shut her down can't bode well for anyone.

110

Judge Supreme Martine clears her throat and turns to face the remaining members of the Coalition, then back to the crowd of Humans and Regonians.

"It seems we have more to address," she whispers, voice hoarse and rasping over the words.

Martine draws in a shaky breath, and my heart hammers. She puts a hand to her chest, then looks up at us.

"We've been presented with… evidence of past crimes," she forces herself to say. "Robert Mulvaney, I'll need you to rise with Eva Dobovich once more."

The soldiers assigned to him train their weapons on him as he hauls himself up.

"Bolivia Station…" Martine says.

Mulvaney glares at Olivia, eyes burning with rage.

But when Eva looks at her daughter, when she sees the empty look in Olivia's eyes, Eva buckles. She drops her gaze, face crumpling.

Bolivia Station?

The words mean nothing to me, but they send my heart skipping. With Humans, the unknown is very much a thing to fear.

Chapter Eleven
Termana

Olivia

My mother meets my gaze for half a heartbeat, but I haven't the energy to glare at her, not now. The fresh horrors of her actions wash through me, anesthetizing me to the world.

Because I still see them.

In my mind, the lights on Bolivia Station flicker once, then go dark. Screams ring out, echoing through metal halls. But mother sits quietly, calm in her office, watching streams of data scroll on one screen as another screen showcases Bolivia Station.

As she pumped the air out.

After her illegal tests failed.

Here and now, her eyes fall to the floor, flinching before me.

She clearly feels no shame over experimenting on Regonians, for killing so many of them. But perhaps she feels shame over committing those same atrocities against Humans.

My eyes shift out of focus, and the world fades in and out around me. The hearing over Bolivia Station passes in a blur. My hands tremble in my lap, so I clench them into fists, trying to block it all out.

But I know where this leads.

With footage of her crimes against the Regonians and our own people alike, with full confessions to the former… There's only one punishment the Coalition can extend, former Ministers or not.

"Miss Olivia Dobovich?" Judge Martine's voice chimes, drawing my attention. "There is one last matter to address before we move to sentencing."

Thousands of eyes fall on me, and my blood runs cold. I squirm as I rise to my feet. My heart races, and I wait for something terrible, even though they sat me with the Regonians, not with those on trial.

My stomach lurches.

"There is the matter of Atlantis," Judge Martine says. "The security program you installed across every Human system."

Whispers course through the crowd, and my palms sweat.

"Do you feel you should be on trial here?" Judge Martine asks.

I swallow nervously, eyes dropping as she continues.

"You took down security protocols in favor of something untested. You risked lives. Why should we trust that you won't commit crimes like your mother's? Do you have anything to say for yourself?"

I flinch at her accusation that I might be anything like my mother. Clearing my throat, I search for words.

Eventually, I say, "I never risked any more lives than we were already risking. All the old security systems are still online. I left them up as a failsafe. I'm not so arrogant as to think myself, or my work, infallible."

I stare at my trembling fingers, wishing for a drink to take the edge off. Tears fill my eyes, blurring the world. "Believe me, I know my shortcomings."

"Good. Then, you'll face no criminal charges," Judge Martine says, pulling a sigh of relief from me. "But there is a

114

condition. If we're all standing when this is over, you must take up a position that utilizes your skills. Cleaning bathrooms will no longer cut it. You must finally rise to your potential."

Or fall short…

I give her a sheepish nod.

Judge Martine nods in return, dismissing me. I sit, nearly collapsing into my chair under the weight of all the eyes still resting upon me.

But the honorable judge speaks again, addressing Tenna and Krona.

And all those eyes desert me.

Chapter Twelve
Termana

Tenna

Judge Martine looks to Krona and I, eyes softening. "Is there anything that the King and Queen of Daen Tribe would like to say in these matters?"

We rise to our feet in unison, heads held high. Our hands twine together, but our eyes never leave Judge Martine's face.

"We have three demands," I say. I speak in our tongue, letting the translators do their job. "We expect the immediate and total reversal of all experiments performed on those of us *who yet live*."

Krona squeezes my hand, lending me his strength as I continue.

I say, "We demand safe transport home."

I pause, letting them wait for this final demand. The Human side of the room stills, all eyes on the *alien* queen.

My stomach coils tight with rage as my brother's death flashes before my eyes for the hundredth time since I remembered it just this morning. My free hand curls into a tight fist.

"As for all those who were party to these *depraved* proceedings," I hiss, "I. Demand. Death. No one slaughters my people and lives. Either you order their death, or I will."

To my left, my mother, father, and sister rise to their full heights. They stomp their right feet. Once, twice, three times. On Krona's right, his parents rise, joining mine for three more soul shattering stomps.

Behind us, auditorium chairs groan as just over 4,000 Regonians rise, beating the floor in steady, rhythmic stomps. Only Krona and I stand motionless, a dam holding back a roiling tsunami of rage and sorrow.

Messages flash across the Coalition members' Links in an urgent shade of yellow. Their faces darken with the realization of just how tenuous our control is over our people's fury. Shadows move behind their eyes.

Are they tallying the devastation we could wreak upon them?

They've seen just a handful of Regonians stand against a horde of their elite Soldiers, with Krona and I the only trained warriors among them. We suffered two casualties.

And we left no survivors.

Judge Supreme Martine meets my gaze, and her voice whispers into my mind through my cochlear implant. "We've reached our decision."

Krona and I raise our free hands, and our Tribe stills behind us. Silence falls in the wake of their furious movements, heavy and thick with tension.

"The deaths of those who did this were never in question," she says, voice low and firm. "And we readily agree to your other terms. Any and all experiments will be reversed immediately, and you'll be provided safe passage home. We'll have to prepare our ships, but as soon as they're ready, we'll see to it that you make it home. I don't know how funerals are handled on Regonia, but if you'd like, we can put your loved ones in cryo-storage so they can be mourned properly when you get there."

I dip my chin in a slow nod.

This surprising bit of thoughtfulness reminds me that not every Human here is a vicious traitor. It reminds me that there are victims in their ranks, as well. For though I don't know exactly what happened on Bolivia Station, I surmised enough from the hearing to know there were many Human casualties.

In their tongue, I say, "So, it shall be."

Behind Judge Supreme Martine, Minister Croon speaks up. "We tracked the trajectory of the man who died on Odyssey, the first death. If you'd like us to recover him so that he may be mourned properly as well, we can."

A lump forms in my throat.

"Please do. His ashes should nourish our land, and his family should have the chance to find his sound."

And a thought strikes me.

"There is one more thing," I say. "On Regonia, it would go without saying. Here, I cannot assume. The executions and funerals of those who have been sentenced today must be silent. Not a single word may be uttered. Their sounds must go unsought, lost and without the honor of crossing another's lips."

Judge Martine nods. "It shall be done."

Behind me, the remnants of Daen Tribe whisper amongst themselves for half a breath, then take their seats. The poor chairs groan beneath their weight, unused to supporting such heavy beings.

Krona's family sits next. Then, my own family settles in.

As Krona and I sit, Mr. Croon rises to his feet. Judge Supreme Martine bows her head toward the crowd, then takes her seat, relinquishing the stage.

A single gesture beckons innocent guards and soldiers to come forward. They stand ready as the prisoners rise from their seats. Restraints clink together, a soft, discordant chaos ringing in my ears.

Another gesture sees the condemned marched out of the auditorium with heads hanging low, shamed by hate-filled glares on all sides or weighed down by the death sentence they received. Mulvaney's gaze bores holes in the back of the soldier before him.

Only one head rises above the sea of people. Eva Dobovich searches the crowd, eyes finally coming to rest on their target. I turn, tracing her gaze.

But Olivia stares at her lap, refusing to meet her mother's eyes. Tears tremble on her lashes. A few tracks shine on her cheeks.

Guilt burns hot inside me, not for demanding justice. But for hurting Olivia by demanding her mother's death.

I wouldn't change it, wouldn't undo what I've done this day. Justice must be served. Lives were taken unjustly, and they must be paid for.

But that never makes the casualties easier to bear.

I look back at Eva, glancing over my shoulder to do so. She walks calmly, giving her guards no trouble. But her gaze never leaves her daughter.

Chapter Thirteen
Termana

Krona

The Humans all file out, and silence settles in their wake. The Survival Coalition looks to us, and Tenna and I rise to our feet.

Minister Croon pulls in a deep breath. "There are still matters to discuss," he begins, gray hair shining in the harsh light. "Work is underway, situating the housing sections of Beijing and Venice Stations for your Tribe."

A wave of unease ripples through our people, prickling the hairs on the back of my neck. Nausea builds within me.

They intend to separate us?

"The cafeterias will return to their intended purpose for the duration of your stay," Croon continues. When nervous whispers move through our people, muttered misgivings shifting in the air, he hastens to add, "Everything will be done to return you to your homes as soon as possible, but you need a decent place to sleep in the meantime."

But he soothes the wrong problem.

They've already agreed that we'll be taken home as soon as can be made possible, and we made clear what we could do if they go back on their word.

So, I clear things up for him. "Is there no way for us to avoid separating? Can we not stay on a single Station?"

"I suppose you could stay on one Station. It'll be cramped, though. They're not meant to hold so many people at a time. But I suppose we could put beds in the gym and the store. If we use some of the bunks from the… experiments…" Croon rubs a weary hand over his face. "We could fit more of you into each room that way, stacking them like bunk beds."

He meets my eyes, brows furrowed. "Would you prefer that? If you need time to discuss, that's fine."

But I feel the way the air shifts around us as relief gusts from our people, hear the words they whisper in our tongue. I glance at Tenna, and she nods once.

Turning around, I cast my gaze over our people. They sit, leaning into one another over tiny armrests, hands clasped together. A few couples face each other, foreheads bowed together. Their hands rest upon each other's cheeks.

Swallowing, I nod and turn back around.

"We stay together."

Croon accepts this decision, sending out a flurry of messages from his Link. The screen blinks softly each time another message leaves him.

"It'll be done," he says. "But there's still one thing that begs our attention. We must decide what to do about the Drennar."

I almost tell him that they're his problem, almost hope that Tenna will say as much.

But that isn't altogether true, and we all know it.

The Drennar lied to us. They told us tales of star-sickness, then abandoned us, only to look on from afar.

Watching us.

Our lives, our customs, our world is not what we thought it was.

And we deserve answers.

"I assume you'd still like to discuss matters here?" Croon asks.

Tenna and I nod.

"The Drennar have been taking Humans for nearly forty years," Croon says. "And they show no sign of stopping any time soon. We have no idea how long they monitored us before they started abducting our people."

A deep, sick feeling brews in my stomach.

How long have the Drennar been watching us? Since they left us on Regonia?

Will they start abducting us, too?

Croon carries on without noticing my trepidation. Tenna notices, as she always does, and squeezes my hand.

"With Olivia's program, Atlantis, in place, we hope the abductions will slow or stop altogether. Only time will tell. But I fear that our best chance might be to go on the offensive. We know where they are, and... electricity is likely a weakness of theirs as well..." Croon's shoulders fall with a deep sigh.

"But we may well need your help. I labor beneath no delusions. Our tech falls short of theirs. Our physical might falls far shorter. But yours does not. And though it isn't your war yet, there's no way to know if the Drennar will come for your people in the future as they have done for ours."

Hearing my fear spoken aloud, my heart pounds unsteadily in my chest.

"We must fight back," Croon says. "Together. An alliance may be the only way to stop the Drennar from taking more Humans or to prevent them from taking Regonians."

Tenna grips my hand tight. "This," she begins, "we must discuss."

***

Olivia ferries us all to Venice Station. Tenna exchanges a tearful, yet strained goodbye with her. The Human girl seems lost and broken.

How could she not be?

Her own mother orchestrated the deaths of so many, even turned on her own people.

Olivia disembarks for Odyssey, promising that we'll be taken back to Termana for the executions if we wish. Then, we set ourselves to work arranging our surrounds. Not a single soul among us ventures to the cafeteria, not yet. Tenna and I move through the residential ring, reuniting families.

Then, we meet with the Memory Markers to discuss a new tattoo to mark so much pain, so much loss, for such an event as this cannot be born only by the normal marks. Those will be administered as well, of course, to mark us all with those we've lost.

But our cores have been shaken.

Our lives are different now.

And that cannot go unmarked.

Chapter Fourteen
Novay

Rone

My pedestal glows before me, signaling the successful submission of my proposal. Reviewing all that I've sent, my stomach flips. Hope burns inside me.

And yet, my heart twists.

With a thought, I dismiss my podium, watching as the alonarium ripples with minute electrical currents and sinks back into the floor. I move away, meandering back to my quarters, but my steps lack the cool efficiency of my peers. They brush past me with ease, off to participate in or oversee their assigned experiments, or perhaps to rest for their allotted three hours.

But my steps are halting, arms swinging awkwardly at my sides. It's time for me to rest, but too many emotions swirl within me. A sigh lifts my shoulders.

Will they let me break his solitude?

Again, I pull up my proposal, sweeping through it in my mind as grey walls blur around me. I check over every data point, every aspect of his experiment. I analyze the experiments of the other subjects, Chrissy, Nicolai, and Yuri.

They've all been alone for roughly the same length of time. They've been subjected to similar tests, and pulling them from their current experiments won't lower the number of people in those experiments enough to negatively impact the outcome.

The new experiment, the reintroduction to other Humans, should be acceptable. With so few, it would be a good sample to see if the experiment is worth pursuing on a larger scale.

At my quarters, the wall slides back for me instantly, recognizing my sync signature. I step through, letting it close behind me, not bothering to turn on my lights. I know the exact distance to my bed. I calculate the width of each stride, measuring it against my normal strides to weigh the impact of my emotions.

I think of Reginald's face when he sees another Human, alive and present, for the first time in twelve years, and a smile plasters itself over my face.

Yet, my heart sinks.

What if...

What if he likes one of the Human women better than me?

What if he doesn't want to talk to me or hold my hand or... kiss me?

I pull in a deep breath and crawl into my bed, curling in on myself as my chest collapses. My wings flutter behind me, restless and taking it out on the air. I ignore the knowledge that all the other Drennar who left the facility center with me are asleep already, that *I* should be asleep already.

But my mind is full of Reginald's face. His smile, the one that's been reserved for me lately, beams at another Human. His lips meet hers, and I hear a soft moan to the tune of Chrissy's voice, pulled from footage from her life before, as my mind acts of its own accord to torment me in a way it never did before.

My shoulders shake with a small sob.

But this will be better for Reginald. For Chrissy, Nicolai, and Yuri, too.

They'll be happier.

Berating myself, I try desperately to forget these emotions and get some rest. I fully exerted myself today, stretching my mind to analyze all potential data points for so many experiments, trying desperately to find one that might work, and now, exhaustion tugs at me, weakening my control over my emotions. Tears fall freely at the prospect of losing Reginald to someone else, even if it's better for him.

The response comes, and three blinks of my ears illuminate my room. A wave of ice water sweeps over me, and every muscle in my body tenses.

Another thing we thought was mere hyperbole.

I check the decision my peers have come to, and selfish relief washes over me, warring with the anguish I feel on his behalf.

I won't lose him to another Human because he'll still be alone.

Tears leak from my eyes, and I squirm internally, hating how relieved I am to have this proposal rejected, even if I'm also disappointed. I barely register the reason for the rejection, barely note the fact that they have plans for Reginald's immediate future.

And yet, I can't help but wonder.

Would he still want me if he had a choice?

Does it matter that I tried to give him one?

Chapter Fifteen
Realm of Stars

Ricardo

On the ship back to Odyssey, Olivia sits pensive in the captain's chair. She stares out at the stars, reverent and awestruck.

But she looks so small before the vast abyss.

Her once luscious tawny skin seems pale in the light of the control panels. Her smooth dark hair hangs limp in a ponytail. Space seems to reach in through the giant window to swallow her up.

I tear my eyes away from her as Odyssey comes into view. Taking my seat behind her, I strap in. After all, she's a good pilot, but she's been out of it lately. I'd rather not have my feet taken out from under me if she sets us down a little roughly.

But when the airlock opens before us, she guides the ship in as easily as breathing. We touch down, soft and gentle.

The turntable beneath the ship spins us around to face the exit as I unbuckle. Olivia flips switches and turns dials, barely looking at her hands as she moves. But the outer door of the airlock doesn't close.

I tip my head to the side.

Is there a problem with the door?

But Olivia unbuckles, regardless. Rising, she approaches the big window at the front of the ship, placing one hand against it. A song bursts from the speakers throughout the room, loud and sudden, startling me. I glance at my Link.

"Angel by Tokio Myers. 2017."

I approach her on unsteady legs. If she notices the sound of my footsteps buried within the mournful piano, she doesn't acknowledge it.

"I'm sorry, Dad," she whispers to the stars, and I stop in my tracks. A sob shakes her frame so hard I fear it may break her. "I'm sorry," she says again.

My throat goes tight, closing around a lump. "Olivia, this isn't your fault," I tell her, voice hoarse.

She pulls in a deep, shuddering breath, leaning her head against the window. Finding my courage, I walk toward her, put a hand on her back.

Drawing up beside her, I let my eyes roam over her profile. Tears stain her cheeks, falling to splatter at her feet. Her eyes fall shut, hiding brilliant hazel from the worlds.

"It is my fault though," she says, voice so small I barely hear her over the building music. "I should've kept a closer eye on her. I should've finished Atlantis sooner, but I didn't. And now…"

Shaking her head, Olivia holds back another sob. "2,068 Regonians are dead. She killed them." A little sob escapes her. "Then, I killed 506 Humans. Sure, they're not dead yet, but they will be. Because of me. Had I finished Atlantis sooner, none of this would've happened."

Pain lances my chest.

She actually believes this is her fault.

Spinning her to face me, I take her face in my hands. "Olivia, this was *not* your fault. Those 506 people decided their own fate. You didn't kill *anyone*."

I ask my Link a quick favor, coming up with exact figures, and say, "You *saved* 4,117 lives. And with all your work on Odyssey, warning civilians and locking doors so those assholes would have to stop and enter their credentials… You saved who knows how many lives here."

A deep, soul-shaking sob bursts from her, and I pull her into my arms. She folds into me, curling in on herself as her tears soak my shirt.

"You didn't kill anyone," I whisper, forcing the words past a lump in my throat. I put one hand to the back of her head, cradling her against my chest. "If there was any way to tell him, your dad would be *proud* of you."

Olivia's hands ball into fists around the fabric of my shirt. Her body shakes, and the tears become a torrential downpour. The song starts over, soaking us in the sad notes of a piano once more, and her whimpers carry through the cockpit, far clearer with less opposition.

I place a tender kiss on the top of her head, hating that I brought her into this. My heart twists, because I put this weight on her shoulders. Tears prick at the corners of my eyes.

But there was no one else that could've done it.

No one else would have stood half a chance at getting the information we needed or keeping the Soldiers out of people's quarters. No one else could've figured out what was going on.

Or found the footage of Bolivia Station.

So, I wrap my arms tighter around her and let her cry it out. She stands there, gripping the front of my shirt and pouring an ocean of tears into the cockpit. But as the same song swirls around us, over and again, her tears slow.

Eventually, she pulls back, wiping her face, only to stare out at the stars beyond the outer airlock door.

"I barely even remember him," she whispers. "He gave himself up to the Drennar so they wouldn't take me, and I *barely* remember him. I have the memories saved back on my Link from old birthday parties and music recitals. Things I thought were important enough to save before they took him…"

Her brows furrow, and I worry she may start crying again. But how could she have any tears left?

Sitting down on the floor, still staring out at the stars, she asks, "What was your dad like?"

I sigh, desperately wishing I could avoid this topic. Settling down beside her, I look at her before turning my gaze to the stars. "He was shitty. Still is."

And then, I tell her about the abuse I suffered at his hands, the abuse my mother let happen. I tell her about the times I stepped in to spare my little brother from the drunken attacks, and how I fear that I may have shaped my brother into the careless, cruel man he became by shielding him.

Even my mother's drunken stupors fall from my lips, spilling like the liquor bottles she dropped when she passed out.

"Why do parents have to be people?" she asks. "Why can't they just stay parents?"

The stars blink before us as she opens up, unraveling her life, telling me how she raised herself after her father was taken. She tells me about the incessant boredom in school that originally led her to start hacking into her mom's computers.

"I just couldn't believe it…" she says. "She was experimenting on the people on Bolivia Station. I was just… so disappointed. And she's my mom. Kids shouldn't have to be disappointed by their mom, but I was, and now…"

She trails off, staring at the stars with eyes full of sorrow. Her fingers worry at each other in her lap.

Reaching over, I take her hand in mine. Our fingers lace together, and a soft warmth spreads through me. A single tear slips over her cheek, landing on my wrist.

The music slips into the background, falling out of range of my attention. I stare out at the stars, a broken man sitting next to a broken woman, hoping we can put ourselves back together someday.

Chapter Sixteen
Odyssey

Olivia

Ricardo walks me to my room, hand wrapped around mine. Every now and again, he looks at me, staring intently.

But I never meet his gaze.

My eyes glue themselves to the floor, watching the way my feet scuff across the cold surface.

Some small part of me wants to believe him, wants to believe that I did something good. But I know better. I knew Atlantis was important, I knew it could save lives. I should have thrown every waking second into it until it was done, but I didn't.

And people died.

Hundreds. Thousands of people.

Because of me.

The tribunal flashes through my mind, showing me the way my mother looked at me after I turned in the Bolivia footage, and I flinch before the memory. That broken woman, that terrible woman, the woman who never cared for me, the woman who hurt so many people...

Is my mom.

And the apple certainly doesn't fall far from the tree.

We pass a window, and the black hollow of space stares in at me, calling me forward. Numb, I stare back, wondering what it might be like to step out of an airlock without a suit on.

Would I feel the cold?

Or would it be over so quickly I wouldn't even notice it?

We walk further, and the curve of the residential section steals the window from view. My eyes drift back to the ground, and I trudge onward. People walk past, making their way to the cafeteria. A few stare openly, while others have the decency to pretend not to.

But I shrink into myself, regardless.

The door to my room slides open, making me jump. I hadn't even noticed we'd walked so far. Ricardo gathers up his casual clothes and heads into the bathroom.

"I'll change in here," I mumble. "Just... knock, I guess, when you're ready to come out."

"Okay," he says, shutting the door.

I discard my slacks, exchanging them for a pair of black leggings. The button-down shirt and the bra go next. I dig in the bottom of a trunk at the foot of my bed, freeing one of my dad's old t-shirts. I press the dark grey fabric to my face, breathing it in.

But it hasn't smelled like him in years.

It smells like me and my room, like old books and too much alcohol.

Ricardo knocks from within the bathroom, and I say, "One second." I tug the shirt over my head and pull my hair through the neck. "Okay. You can come out, now."

Stowing his clothes in a little drawer I cleared out for him, Ricardo glances at me with furrowed brows. "Are you not going to dinner?"

I shake my head, and my eyes fall to the floor, faltering before his earnest gaze. "I'm not really hungry."

He clears the distance between us and wraps me in his embrace. Tentatively, I slide my arms around his waist.

But I don't deserve the warmth of his touch.

I don't deserve his comfort.

My lips quiver, and I shout at myself internally.

Just keep it together until he leaves.

Pulling back, Ricardo plants a tender kiss on the top of my head. "Do you want me to bring anything back for you?"

I shake my head, still unable to meet his gaze. "I'm just going to get some sleep."

Which isn't necessarily a lie.

"Okay," he says. "Get some rest. It's been a long day."

I nod slowly.

It's been a long life.

But maybe not much longer.

Ricardo turns from me, wandering into the hall and toward the cafeteria. Doubtless, he'll let Maria, Matteo, and Nico know not to worry about me.

Turning back to the trunk at the foot of my bed, I pull a dark bottle free. I don't bother with a glass. I don't bother savoring my favorite whiskey.

Tipping the bottle up, I take one swig after another, begging it to burn away the sight of so many dead Regonians, or the dead Humans on Bolivia Station. My throat burns, and my stomach grows warm. The alcohol spreads through me, a comforting angel in the midst of my own personal hell.

But I keep drinking.

One long gulp after another, I try desperately to forget. When the bottle holds nothing more than droplets, I let it fall from my grasp. It lands with a solid thunk on the rug and falls over.

For a moment, I simply stand there, waiting for it to take hold of me. I stare at the things I've collected over the years, letting my gaze roam lovingly over the shelves. Stepping forward, I run a hand over the spines of a few books, tracing the edges of the letters.

My mind begins to quiet. The alcohol obscures the dead bodies, blurring them into a single, inhuman monstrosity. Which isn't necessarily better. The world before me drifts in and out of focus as my head spins.

Making my way back to the trunk, I dig for one little bottle. It rests in the very bottom, shoved away months ago out of shame. But now, I need it.

My hand finds it, pulling it free of the trunk. The world slips to the side, and the bottle's contents rattle within it as I nearly fall over. Pulling on a jacket, I stash the bottle in my pocket, and do something I've never done.

I head to the hangar with alcohol sloshing in my veins. I even grab a small bottle of whiskey from the drawer of my nightstand as I make my way out of my room.

My feet carry me, stumbling and angling through empty halls. With everyone busy eating in the cafeteria, I fumble my way through the station unnoticed. The floor tips beneath me, sending me wobbling toward a wall.

But I push onward.

At the door to the hangar, my Link grants me access. After all, I'm still a pilot. For now.

I venture through, eyes roaming lovingly over the two ships before me. Forsaking the larger one, the one that ferried me to the tribunal to condemn my own mother and receive forgiveness I shouldn't have gotten, I seek out SCCS Sparrow. She's carried me into the stars so many times, showing me peace over and again.

More times than I deserve.

I run a shaking hand over her metal exterior, stopping to lean against her when the whiskey tips the floor beneath me. Slow progress leads me to the hatch, and my Link lowers it for me.

As more and more of the alcohol soaks into my system, I move slower, trying hard not to fall on the ramp into Sparrow. It takes a moment, but I manage, hauling myself up into the small cargo bay.

Seats line the outer edges, waiting for passengers that I'll never ferry again. Bars recessed into the floor wait for straps to hold cargo in place. But I'll never fasten them down again.

A tear falls, streaking over my skin.

"I'll miss you, old girl," I whisper to Sparrow. But she's powered down. Her OS doesn't hear me.

Tottering through the ship, I climb a few small stairs and pass through another door that my Link accesses for me.

And there it is.

My seat. My safe place.

A million buttons and dials and knobs and levers await, begging me to take her out for one last flight.

Begging me to never come back, to disappear into the stars with Sparrow.

And what would I have to come back to anyway?

A genocidal mother that never cared enough about me to take a day off? How long do I have her before she's executed? One day? Two?

I can't exactly come back for my dad.

Or Ricardo.

Another tear falls.

Again, I hear him say I saved lives, but I know the truth. My heart clenches painfully in my chest because I know I could have prevented their deaths. I could have prevented all of this.

And I can't stomach the disappointment I know will haunt his face when he finally realizes that.

I'm just like her...

Turning on Auxiliary power with a single switch, I have my Link play some music for my final time aboard Sparrow.

All I ask it is for the music to be beautiful and peaceful. It doesn't disappoint. Soft, mournful piano seeps from the speakers throughout the cabin as "Arcanine by Ursine Vulpine. 2017." whispers to me from beyond the graves of earth.

I close my eyes, soaking it up.

This is it.

This is my last song.

I tell my Link to play only this one.

An errant thought wonders if my body will reach Earth after I'm jettisoned, if I'll burn up in the atmosphere.

Or if I'll just drift through space forever.

I like that better.

A strange sense of peace fills me at the thought of joining the stars, of floating through their realm for eternity.

I totter toward my seat and topple into it. Then, I signal the turntable, spinning Sparrow and me to face the hatch door. It looms over me, impeding my view. A signal from my Link draws the hatch up, scans the hangar for life, then locks it down. The exterior door rises before me, showing me heaven.

Stars blink and glow and twinkle. Planets hang in the distance, luminous and breathtaking beyond the unmined sections of the asteroid belt.

Pulling the little plastic bottle from my pocket, I ask of the stars and planets beyond, "Keep me with you…"

I twist the lid off and pour a generous handful of antidepressants into my waiting palm. Clumsily, I toss them into my mouth, and a gulp from my tiny bottle of whiskey chases them down.

My Link glows a warm amber, flashing the words, "Messages sent."

But my groggy mind struggles to piece it together.

What messages did I send?

Not that it matters.

I pour another handful of pills, emptying the bottle, and throw them back. After draining the whiskey, I drop both empty bottles to the floor.

Staring at the stars, I wonder if my dad is still alive. I wonder what he would've done if the Drennar had taken me, like they planned.

He and mom would've had another kid. They would've moved on.

My thoughts fracture.

Mom never would have…

I never would have…

I sigh.

But when my eyes blur, it isn't from tears. I don't need to cry anymore. I lean back in my seat, then sit still to keep the nausea at bay. The whiskey and the pills rise up, trying so hard to drag me under.

But I keep my eyes open, watching the stars as long as I can.

"I'm sorry, Dad," I whisper when my eyes finally close. "I should've been so much better."

Chapter Seventeen
Odyssey

Ricardo

Draining the last of my water, I smile at a joke Nico made. Yet, I can't shake the conversation with Olivia just before dinner. Something about her seemed different. She cried, yes, but... She actually talked to me.

That isn't exactly like her.

A wistful smile plays over my lips at the intimacy of it. I can only hope she'll see reason, that she'll realize that this wasn't her fault, no matter how long it took her to finish Atlantis.

Making the program at all was more than most people were doing. And far *better* than what anyone else was doing.

I haven't heard of any new abductions since she put that program into effect a few days ago. It might be coincidence. Maybe they're not taking people right now.

Or maybe she's managed to block their access to us.

If anyone could do it, it'd be her.

My heart warms. I smile, far more genuinely than the one my lips played host to at Nico's joke.

Because I'm proud of her.

Even setting aside the silly, schoolboy crush I had on her when I first came here and the drunken, stressed-out sex that first night, taking those things completely out of the equation… I'm genuinely proud of her. And though I know she has problems, alcoholism to start with, I want to spend time with her.

I want to get to know her better.

Fuck, I want to help her through this.

Realization dawns on me.

Am I falling for her?

But life affords me no further time to puzzle out the answer.

My Link flashes an angry red, over and over. And so does Maria's.

I glance down to find a message from Olivia. All it says is, "Help."

My heart plummets, and my mouth goes dry.

As soon as the Link registers that I've seen the message, it shifts, showing me a map of the station with a big red dot over SCCS Sparrow in the hangar. I meet Maria's eyes over the table, just long enough to realize that she's gotten the same message. Fear shines in her eyes, glistening on a sheen of tears.

And then, I'm on my feet, sprinting for the hangar with my heart in my throat.

My palms sweat as I push through small crowds, feet slamming against the floor, desperate to get to her. My Link still flashes an angry red, casting an eerie glow on the walls as I charge through the station. People jump out of my way, startled and affronted, but I don't give a damn.

The last time she messaged me asking for help...

I shudder as the sight of Lachlan choking her flickers through my mind, and I push myself harder. I skip the elevator, unwilling to wait on it to greet me.

My Link scans at the door to the stairs, granting me access, and I fly down them, hopping over two and three steps at a time, willing myself not to trip.

Please, don't let me be too late.

I burst through the door at the bottom of the stairs. Two Guards talk near the door to the hangar, both with plates of food in hand. I remember them in line ahead of me in the cafeteria and wonder how long they've been away from their post.

My eyes scan ahead, seeking out the porthole that allows a view of the hangar.

Why is the exterior door open?

I shout ahead, "SHUT THAT DOOR!"

One of the Guards jumps, spilling her food.

"SHUT THE GODDAMN DOOR!" I scream, voice bordering on hysteria.

Spinning on her heel, she peers through the porthole and exclaims, "What the…?"

But they're not moving fast enough. I draw up even with them and rush into their office. The clean white walls close in on me.

Behind their desk, I scan my Link at the computer, but it does nothing. I don't have clearance for a hangar.

Strong arms grab me, jerking me away from the computer. The male Guard slams me against the wall, shouting in my face.

But the female goes to the computer and scans in.

I push the man off me, sending him toppling over the chair behind the desk. He almost takes out the woman, but she keeps her footing long enough. I hear the exterior door slide shut, feel the movement of it vibrating the walls.

"Get me in there," I demand, already moving for the door.

But the man springs to his feet, grabbing me from behind.

156

"Where the fuck do you think you're going? You just assaulted a Guard."

But I'm beyond caring.

I slam him into the wall, shouting, "I don't fucking care." My arm pins his neck, and I hiss, "Olivia's in there. Get me in."

Realization dawns on him, just as the woman behind me says, "It's pressurizing."

I shove away from the man and sprint toward the airlock door. My fists beat against it, shouting, "Olivia!"

But I know she won't hear me.

Not inside Sparrow.

Please, let her be inside Sparrow…

Not out in space…

The door hisses open at an agonizing pace, and I squeeze through before it opens completely. I charge Sparrow, and one of the Guards lowers her hatch before I get there, filling the hangar with the music that blares inside the ship. Vaulting up the ramp, I duck into the cargo bay.

But there's no sign of Olivia.

Keep moving. She's here.

Moving further, I call out, "Olivia?"

Fear trickles down my spine, riding on beads of sweat. I step into the cockpit.

And there she is.

Her arms hang limp over the sides of the captain's chair.

An empty pill bottle rests on the floor on one side of her. An empty alcohol bottle lays on her other side. My stomach drops.

Oh, god no…

Rushing forward, I kneel before her, staring at her slack face. "Oh, god, Olivia. No, you can't do this."

I pat her face, desperate for some reaction, but she doesn't move.

What do I do?

My heart hammers behind my ears, drowning out nearly everything. The Guards appear in the door to the cargo bay, hands slipping up to cover their open mouths.

"Olivia, no. NO! You can't do this. Please…" My voice wavers, breaking over tears.

Pulling her from the chair, I settle her on the floor. I shout at the Guards, desperate for help. The woman approaches slowly.

"What do you need?" she asks, quiet and scared.

"Hold her up," I say, leaning Olivia forward. She hangs in my arms like a puppet. Her skin nearly burns me. The Guard slides her arms around Olivia, and I crouch in front of her limp form.

I tip her head up, and her jaw falls open.

Oh my god, oh my god, oh my god…

Hating it even as I do it, loathing the feel of Olivia's teeth scraping the backs of my knuckles and the top of my hand, I stick one finger down her throat. She gags, and a mess of lunch, alcohol, and far too many pills comes up.

I wipe my hand on my pants and scream at the male Guard to call a doctor.

"Olivia, you can't leave like this. Please," I beg.

But she doesn't respond.

The woman holding her up weeps openly, but never lets Olivia fall. "Is she dead?" she asks, eyes full of tears.

"NO. She's not dying. She's NOT!" I say, demanding that the universe listen to me. "She is NOT dying." Then, my voice breaks as I add, "She can't."

Scooping her up in my arms, damning the mess, I carry her out of Sparrow. Running through the hangar, I whisper, "Olivia, please… You can't. You can't die."

Cold metal halls blur as I run, but Olivia merely lolls in my arms.

Then, I hear it. A single sound, one lonely siren, wails in the corridor. It echoes off the walls, beating my eardrums.

And I push faster.

My feet pound the floors, drowning out even the frantic drumming of my heart. I round a corner and see them.

Dr. Sullivan, a nurse, and a woman I don't know all sit in a motorized cart, careening toward me. My heart flutters, hoping they're not too late. Slowing my pace to keep from slamming into them, I start to explain what happened.

But the woman I don't recognize says, "We know. Just set her on the stretcher."

Dr. Sullivan is already out, unfolding the stretcher from the back of the cart. I lay Olivia down upon it as gently as I can. The nurse comes over, shining a flashlight into Olivia's eyes as Dr. Sullivan digs in his pack, pulling out a small needle.

But the woman I don't know pulls me away.

I tug my arm loose from her grasp, reaching for Olivia, begging, "Please. Don't do this."

But soft hands grab my face, turning me away from Olivia.

"You did good," the strange woman says. "You did everything you could. Now, it's their turn, okay?"

My eyes well up with tears, and my face scrunches up. Our conversation this afternoon floats through my mind, and I know why she opened up.

Because she didn't have anything to lose.

A sob bursts from my lips. "Oh my god…" I whisper, voice breaking.

"Hey, I need you to focus for just a second, okay?" the strange woman asks. Her dark brown eyes peer into mine, calm but somehow urgent at the same time. "How many pills did she take, do you know?"

"I don't… I don't know. The bottle was empty."

"Okay. That's okay. How many times did she throw up? How much?"

"Just once… I… I made her. Her teeth scraped my hand, and it just felt wrong, and…" A sob rasps through me, cutting off my words.

Beside me the nurse recites Olivia's vitals for Dr. Sullivan. They move in calm unison over Olivia's slack form, as if they've rehearsed this exact scenario, but my breath comes in shallow bursts, choking me rather than soothing me. My lungs seem to convulse in my chest as hyperventilation claims me.

"How about we sit down?" the nice woman with the kind eyes suggests, and I practically collapse.

My hands shake in my lap.

"My name is Cait," the woman before me says.

She kneels, looking so calm, so poised, despite the commotion the nurse and Dr. Sullivan still make, despite Olivia's unconscious form. My eyes drift, just in time to see Dr. Sullivan lock eyes with the nurse and nod.

What does it mean?

Is she going to be okay?

Or is it too late?

"Ricardo?" Cait calls my attention away, and by her tone, I can only assume she's tried several times. "I'm Olivia's counselor. She hasn't been to see me in a while though. She was doing very well when we last spoke, so it seemed natural for her to stop her sessions."

A frown tugs at her lips.

"It would seem she's been having difficulties again."

Difficulties? I'd say this is more than just fucking difficulties.

I gape at her, but she continues, unperturbed.

Does anything ruffle this woman?

162

I guess she wouldn't be very good at her job if she startled easily…

"I'm sure I already know the answer to this, but did Olivia mention the message you received? Before tonight, I mean."

I shake my head.

"I thought as much. Well, anytime a client presents with suicidal thoughts, I request that they program a distress call of sorts into their Link. A few actually," she says, dropping her dark eyes to her hands. "Olivia agreed to program her Link to notify me if she thought about suicide, even just an intrusive thought, but I guess she took that out. Maybe thinking herself a burden…"

She glances at Olivia, and my eyes follow.

Rich, supple skin seems sallow and drawn. Dark, glossy hair hangs lifeless over the edge of the stretcher. Her eyes hide behind closed lids, still determined to shut out the worlds.

"But she kept the distress call. When she…" Cait trails off and clears her throat. I tear my eyes from Olivia only to find a tear slipping over Cait's smooth umber skin. "Five automated messages were sent out. One went to the hospital, and one went to me. Those contained a brief message, her location, and the method by which she… tried to take her life."

I choke back a sob, and my eyes dart to Olivia.

Please, stay with me…

My silent plea repeats in my mind, but Cait continues.

"For the sake of getting someone to her in time, in case someone was closer than we were, the other three were programmed to go to the three people she felt closest to at the time of her attempt."

My jaw drops, and I stare at the counselor. Brows furrowed, I wait for her to go on, but she sits quietly, waiting me out. Turning my attention back to Olivia, I see a small flutter of eyelids, but nothing more.

"She trusts you, Ricardo," Cait tells me. "And I can see why. You did right by her today."

Maria rounds the corner with tears streaking her face. Matteo keeps pace with her, begging her to slow down for the babies, despite the worry that creases his brows and pulls his lips downward.

"Is she okay? Please, tell me she's okay," Maria begs, voice catching painfully.

Maria and I got a message.

Who got the third?

Chapter Eighteen
Venice Space Research Station

Tenna

Earlier that day

Gathered in the cafeteria, unfortunately the only place on the station large enough to hold even half of us, our people wait for Krona and me. We stand in the kitchen with our families and the remnants of our highest ranks, piecing things together.

Murmurs of unease spread through the crowd. People cling to one another, desperate for contact in the face of such loss. With justice decided upon for the wicked, some of the tension faded, but the proposed alliance quickly stirred everyone into a frenzy again.

At long last, I look to Krona. Those magnificent mint green eyes stare back at me, the eyes I never forgot even when the rest of my memories were ripped away. A gentle smile touches his lips.

Taking his hand in mine, I duck through the doorway into the cafeteria. Our people fall silent, waiting for our verdict.

After a short greeting and praise for the justice we'll have in the executions, we move to the topic at hand.

"Whispers abound. Speculation and fear run rampant," I say. "Because we don't know if this is our war or not."

My voice softens as I add, "It's always been clear before."

The crowd before me huddles closer, linking arms and leaning heads on shoulders. They band together in the face of the unknown.

And my heart warms.

"The Vaerkin Tribe has always been a clear enemy, hostile and fiercely territorial. Roon Tribe has never been friendly, but the levels of their hostility depended upon their chieftain. Even that is easily understood. Our alliance with Taron Tribe has been in place for generations. But this..."

I sigh, and Krona squeezes my hand.

"So many aspects of our lives are in a state of upheaval. Our ancestors are still alive, watching us and stealing Humans away from their families. Star-sickness isn't some disease, as we were led to believe. Rather, it seems to be greed and the creation of something called technology. We're here, on an alien craft in the Realm of Stars, with a third of our number waiting for their sounds to be found."

"Our songs, our tattoos, our entire way of being has been called into question. All because the Drennar lied to us. They lied, and then, they left us."

Anger sparks in the eyes of those closest to me, and I know my words have hit their mark.

"Their lies do not change who we have become. They do not change the culture we built for ourselves. But they do leave us to wonder. Are they coming back for us, as they have come time and time again for the Humans? Will they steal us from our beds, from the arms of loved ones?"

Fury builds within me at the prospect of losing more lives to the selfish greed of others. My voice rises as I say, "Must we suffer longer? Must we lose more of our families? Must we sit around waiting for them to come for us?"

Murmurs rumble through the crowd, and I dare not stop, dare not lose my momentum.

"I. Say. NO!" The words shake through me, filling me with purpose. Lifting my hand in the air, pulling Krona's along with it, I shout, "WE STRIKE FIRST!"

Krona repeats my words, and our people join him, shouting the words over and again. My heart flutters in my chest, and adrenaline courses through me. If the Drennar were here now, we'd take them all out in a heartbeat.

I feel it in my bones.

We are one.

Our Tribe, though tested beyond our wildest imaginations, stands together.

And we will fight together.

With a gesture from Krona, the crowd settles down, and he speaks. "Any who are not skilled in combat will be transported to Regonia. Our Warriors will be away from home for a long time, longer than ever before."

He fills his voice with fervor, saying, "But this war is for our children and our grandchildren. For we do not know when the Drennar might come for us. It might be tomorrow. It might be fifty summers from now. On this day, we declare war not for ourselves, not for our own lives. We declare war so that the next generation will have a chance. And that is cause enough."

Cheers and hearty agreement rise from our people's lips. Song fills the cafeteria, reclaiming this place, once a place of desperation and helplessness. But now, thousands of voices ring out, mingling war cries with celebration and mourning.

And my heart soars.

I close my eyes, letting the voices of my people soak into my bones.

Oh, how I missed this.

Krona and I quickly join in, reveling in the joy of a decision made and supported. Our voices melt into the melody, becoming a part of something bigger, something better.

As dinner time approaches, our songs quiet, and people drift into the kitchen to prepare food. I slip into the hall, tugging Krona along with me. We stare in at our people, surviving, making the best of things.

I smile at him, thankful to have him by my side. His arms slide around my waist, pulling me close, and I slip my arms around his neck. My fingers tangle in his hair. Heat bursts over my skin as our lips meet, crushing together.

My heart hammers in my ears, begging for his hands to move over every bit of my body. He pushes me back, pressing me against the wall, leaning into me. His lips drift over my neck, leaving tantalizing kisses in their wake.

I squirm against him, desperate for more.

Casting one last glance at the cafeteria, I jerk my head to the side, signaling him to follow me. Giddy, we run through the halls. Hand in hand, smiling and giggling all the while, we round a bend, then careen around a corner.

A cleaning supply closet waits, and we duck inside. Clothing falls away quickly, littering the floor. I trail my fingers over his spine, eliciting a shiver and a moan of pleasure from him. Krona's hands cup and grasp and squeeze my flesh, burning my skin. Heat pools within me, settling in deep.

Our mouths melt together, tongues dancing madly, but it isn't enough. We aren't close enough.

Krona's hands grasp my thighs, lifting me up. I wrap my legs around him, and he presses me against the cold metal wall. It shocks me, but the contrast between that and the fiery heat of his body, his breath on my neck, pushes me that much further into the throes of want.

And he obliges.

Our bodies merge, and sweet trills of pleasure burst through me. Writhing and moaning, we climb higher and higher, aching for release. I arch my back, pressing my breasts against him. Our lips crash together once more, and he moves deeper, faster within me.

Sharp staccato heart beats pound within my chest, and my breath comes in shallow gasps.

Krona meets my gaze, panting, "Hoo kai voo mai." You are my sound.

And I unravel, whimpering his name.

He drives into me one last time, giving way to the heat between us.

Gasping, we settle on the floor. I straddle his lap, sprinkling gentle kisses over his neck. Krona's hands drift softly over the bare skin of my backside, sliding to my thighs. We revel in the feel of having each other, relishing the closeness.

"Hoo kai voo mai," I finally return.

172

We sit together, unburdened, until our stomachs begin to rumble. Only then do we reach for our clothes.

I slide my shirt on and reach for my pants. Krona trails a hand up the outside of my thigh, and I cast him a wicked glance.

"We must eat first," I say. "You'll need your strength."

He laughs, grabbing up his clothes.

But as I pull my pants on, my Link flashes a startling red, casting a frantic shade over the supply closet. My eyes dart to it, only to find a message from Olivia.

"Help."

My heart drops.

The screen quickly morphs to show a map of Odyssey, highlighting one of the spacecraft in the hangar.

What's happened now?

My blood runs cold, chilling me to my core.

I can't get to her. I can't help her. I'm too far.

I do the only thing I can. I send a flurry of messages to everyone that I know on Odyssey. Maria, Matteo, Dr. Sullivan, Nico.

And most importantly, Ricardo.

If anyone can help her, if anyone can save her, it's him.

173

Chapter Nineteen
Novay

Reginald

After yet another day of equations and calculations, Rone leads me back to my room. We tread through the same cold, barren hallway that we've tread every day for twelve years. My muscles ache to run, to move, to *do* something.

I want to see more of Olivia. I want to know that Eva will be brought to justice.

I want to know if Olivia has seen my message yet.

In my mind, I figure up the time it would take for it to arrive with Human technology. Then, I figure up the time for a message sent with Drennar technology.

How long has it been?

It's so hard to keep track of days here. They blur together with a hazy, grey quality.

Rone's wings rustle before me, crystal clear in the fog of my life. She parts the wall and steps aside to let me pass. For a moment, my spirits fall, thinking she may leave immediately.

But her footsteps follow me in.

A smile lifts my lips and crinkles my eyes. My heart flutters.

Sitting on my bed, I pat the blanket beside me, beckoning her to join me. She does so eagerly, leaning against me and letting her head rest on my shoulder.

"Is this normal?" she asks.

I tip my head forward, peering down at her. "What do you mean? Is what normal?"

"It feels like…" she trails off, sitting up to look me in the eye. "When I sit with you, when we talk, when you look at me, it's like… my wings are in my stomach."

I scrunch my brows up, wondering what she could mean. Then, it dawns on me.

I give her butterflies.

Heat spreads through me, warming my skin. I struggle for words, dropping my gaze to my hands. Reaching out, I twine my fingers with hers, lacing them together. My other hand goes to her wrist, trailing up and down.

"It's something that happens when someone… likes someone," I say. "In a romantic or… physical way."

In my periphery, she nods, apparently satisfied with my answer. But I don't look up. I don't trust myself to.

My fingers keep sliding up and down her wrist, tormenting me with the smooth silk of her pale grey skin. She shivers delicately, and I close my eyes.

It's been so long...

And I give her butterflies.

I close my mind off to that line of thinking, trying desperately not to think about her laugh or the sparkle in her eyes. I beg my mind not to fill with the trouble she must have gone through on my behalf to get a message out to Olivia.

I try so hard not to think about what it might feel like to slide my hand into her hair, to touch the side of her head, kept shaved as some sort of memento for the day she got her emotions.

I try not to think of it.

But her weight shifts on the bed.

Gentle fingers lift my chin, and I open my eyes, helpless and desperate to see her. For a moment, she sits nervously. Her green eyes pierce mine, and the blue striations seem to pulse within them.

"Do I put wings in your stomach?" she asks.

Despite myself, I smile. Completely disarmed by her, I nod. "Yes. Yes, you do."

A smile spreads over her lips, and her eyes twinkle. Leaning forward, she presses her lips to mine. My heart races, and I melt into the kiss. My fingers desert their roaming on her wrist, reaching out for her, tracing the memory of her incision before tangling in her dark hair.

Her hand slides down to my chest, and she pushes me back on the bed, following me down. Our lips never part. Fire burns through me, begging for more, aching for touch. I haven't even indulged myself in years, haven't had the heart.

But Rone is here, hot breath breaking on my neck as she kisses my skin. Her hand slides to my stomach, slipping beneath my shirt to trail over sensitive skin.

A moan crosses my lips, and my eyes fall shut.

My hands wander, moving down her sides to her hips. My body strains, begging me to keep going. I grasp her backside, and seriously consider moving my hands around to the front.

And my eyes snap open.

"Wait…" I say. "Are you… Could we even…?"

Rone's hand stills on my chest, fingers tangled in the patch of hair. She looks up at me, tipping her head to the side. "What's wrong?"

"It's just," I swallow, hoping that clearing my throat might also clear my head. "Are we… compatible?"

Smiling, she says, "Yes. I've been modified. Urges for reproduction appeared to be mixed with emotions, so those modifications were done when they gave me emotion."

Her words comfort me, yet send my brain scurrying through millions of thoughts, scrunching up my brows. I marvel at how easily she speaks of major surgery, of completely altering her physical makeup. I'd accepted it when I thought it was just emotion.

But they gave her… a vagina?

Like… A Human one?

My vast ignorance of Drennar anatomy hits me like a lead weight, and I can't help but wonder.

What did she have before?

"How do Drennar typically reproduce?" I ask.

Propping herself up on her elbow, Rone kisses between my eyebrows, trying to ease the tension there. Her fingers play idly in the hair on my chest, moving beneath my pushed-up shirt, but only for an instant.

She slides her hand free of my shirt, letting her palm rest on my chest with the fabric between us.

"Our original reproduction was similar to yours, though less complicated. Less emotion and feeling, more control. But the body parts functioned… similarly. So, the transition wasn't difficult. I simply can't reproduce. For the sake of the experiment, I was rendered infertile."

Her voice drops to a whisper. "I agreed to those terms, before. But I didn't realize what I was giving up. For most Drennar, reproduction isn't an option. We're all tested, constantly. The top 10 percent are selected each year to have their reproductive materials harvested."

She shifts, looking into my eyes as she continues.

"We modify ourselves and our offspring on a genetic level, but selective reproduction aids the betterment of the race. Birth and maturation are such unnecessary procedures. They take so long and require a great deal of energy, so we let our young develop in tanks until they're fully formed, transmitting information to them as they grow. Everyone is essentially born an adult. I just... never expected the maternal drive to be so strong. I used to wonder what all the fuss was about, why humanity never moved to a more streamlined process like we did."

"Because we love our children," I answer. "We love caring for them from day one. We love teaching them their first words, seeing them take their first steps. There's a bond there that we just can't give up."

My mind drifts through Olivia's earliest years. I see Eva cradling our perfect little baby in the hospital, sweat plastering her hair to her forehead. Olivia was so small, but she had a full head of hair from the start.

I see her crawling through our house, moving faster than any baby should be capable of, just to get into something she wasn't supposed to mess with. I watch her haul herself up to standing with the help of a table, smiling sweetly. All the major moments, the first lost tooth, her first day of school, her first crush.

And all the little moments that maybe weren't as pivotal but meant just as much. That gleam in her eye when she couldn't wait to tell me about something she'd learned in class. The lemon cookies I loved so much, but she, of course, hated and never missed a chance to playfully wrinkle her nose at.

The way her eyes would flutter closed as I read to her each night when she was little.

It all plays out in my mind, pulling tears to my eyes. Then, I see the night I was taken, the night I tried to give Olivia a better life. I can almost count the tears streaking her face as the Drennar carried me away.

"What's wrong?" Rone asks.

Only then do I realize that the blanket beneath my head is wet with fallen tears. Streaks of them trail my temples.

"I just miss Olivia. I wish…" My voice breaks. Wiping tears from my face, I try again. "I wish she could've had a better life. I tried…"

Clearing my throat, I cast around desperately for a change of subject. But my mind doesn't stray far. "How was I a suitable substitute for the experiments here? I don't fill the same criteria."

After all, a middle-aged man doesn't react to emotions the same way a teenage girl would. Them agreeing to take me, all those years ago, just doesn't make sense.

I meet Rone's eyes, expecting her to answer quickly, supplying me with some answer I simply hadn't thought of. But she flinches before my gaze.

Staring at my chest, she says, "I don't think you'll like the answer. I think it'll hurt you." She chews at her bottom lip, avoiding my gaze.

I tip her head back, staring into those blue and green eyes. "Please, tell me."

A deep breath puffs out her chest, but she nods. "You weren't a substitute for her, not exactly. There was another man. The two of you were similar in intelligence, age, and background. His daughter was similar to Olivia in those ways."

My heart goes cold.

"He would've been taken. She wouldn't have. But you were willing to submit, so they took you in his place… and his daughter in Olivia's place."

My jaw falls open, and my throat closes. Fresh tears flow.

Someone else's daughter was taken instead…

For half a heartbeat, my treasonous mind wonders if Olivia would have fared better here, if that other man's wife wouldn't have devolved into a genocidal maniac in his absence.

But I shove the thought away.

"You're hurt…" Rone whispers. Shame burns in her words.

She nestles into me, wrapping her arm around my torso. I wrap my arms around her, planting a gentle kiss on the top of her head.

"Do you ever tire of being right?" I croak, trying to lighten the mood but failing.

"Only recently."

Chapter Twenty
Odyssey Space Research Station

Ricardo

Behind me, Dr. Sullivan whispers, "She's stable."

Relief washes over me, and I push myself up to my feet. Scrambling to Olivia's side, I take her hand in mine. The nurse steps aside, dropping instruments into a small case at the end of the cart labeled "biohazard."

I stare down at the drawn face before me, motionless in unconsciousness. But Olivia's chest rises and falls in smooth, even breaths.

My heart shrivels at the thought that maybe Olivia doesn't realize how much we all want her here.

How much we need her.

A sob wrenches my attention away from Olivia, and my eyes refocus on Maria. Matteo pulls her into his arms, whispering, "She's okay, now. She's going to make it."

"Come see me in the morning, and we'll talk about this," Cait tells her, smoothing the pregnant woman's hair. "For now, go get some rest."

"Not yet," she whispers, pulling away from her husband. She sidles up next to Olivia and reaches out. Putting a tender hand on her friend's cheek, she says, "You're not allowed to leave me."

Fresh tears well up in her eyes, and my own prickle with the promise of rain. She glances at my hand, tangled with Olivia's, then meets my gaze.

"Thank you," she whispers, voice breaking.

I try to form words, but my mouth works uselessly. So, I just give her a solemn nod.

Turning from me, she thanks Dr. Sullivan and the nurse. Matteo touches Olivia's ankle once before turning to put his arm around his wife once more.

As they meander toward the residential section, Cait turns to me. "The other message went to Tenna. I've already contacted her and explained that Olivia is okay, thanks to you. Now, I want you to come see me in the morning, too. You need rest now, but please, come see me."

I nod.

She climbs into the driver's seat of the cart. She casts a glance at me, as if to tell me to venture back to my quarters, but I won't sleep in Olivia's room without her.

I'll stay with her in the hospital tonight.

Sensing my reluctance to leave, she turns the cart on. Dr. Sullivan and the nurse, whose name tag reads *Jessie*, move to the head of Olivia's gurney. Jessie grabs the IV pole, wheeling it along as Dr. Sullivan pushes the gurney.

And I walk alongside them, clutching Olivia's hand.

Chapter Twenty One
Venice Space Research Station

Krona

Tenna paces the floor of our room, humming along with the song that seeps from the speaker, "Little Grave by Chelsea Wolfe. 2019." I drum my fingers on my knee, trying to burn some of this anxious energy out.

But it's useless.

There isn't room here for us to run, to work, to truly exhaust ourselves as we would on Regonia.

Turning to the window, Tenna gazes out at Termana and the space stations dotting her orbit. But which one is Odyssey?

How could Tenna ever know which one to look at? They look exactly the same.

My mind whirls with thoughts of what could have happened.

Another attack, perhaps, perpetrated by someone who slipped our notice? A technical failure of the ship Olivia was in? Some sort of accident? Or was she sick?

She certainly didn't seem to be feeling well when we last saw her.

Abandoning my perch on the side of our bed, I cross the room, drawing up behind Tenna. I slide my arms around her, resting my chin atop her head.

"I'm sure Olivia is alright," I whisper.

Not because I doubt the peril she found herself in. Not because I want to lie simply to placate Tenna. The amount of faith I place in Ricardo shocks me, even as I realize the full breadth of it.

"He'll help her," I say.

A tense nod shakes her in my arms. She slides her hands along my arms, lacing her fingers through mine. "I just wish…" she trails off, voice dropping below the haunting melody floating around us.

But I know.

She wishes she could help, wishes she at least knew what happened.

I know because I wish, too.

But the message said only, "Help."

I remember staring at the word on Tenna's Link, strange Human letters burning in the red glow of the screen. But now, with messages sent to everyone Tenna could think of, with more sent to everyone I could think of, half an hour has passed with no news.

190

I wrap my arms tighter around Tenna, pulling her closer to me. Because there's nothing else I can do. I want to run to Olivia, to this strange little Human girl who's done so much for my people, for Tenna, for me.

But the stars hold me back from her.

How many more would we have lost without her?

I shudder at the thought, and Tenna turns in my embrace. Her hands slide up my chest, coming to rest on the sides of my neck. Humming all the while, she leans her forehead against mine.

She pulls in a deep breath, and so do I.

But a gentle amber glow illuminates the space between us, pulsing softly from Tenna's Link. The worlds all disappear as we focus on that little screen. For the moment, I don't even hate the invasion of it, the fact that we shouldn't have these *things* implanted in us.

Because it brings news of a friend.

Relief washes over Tenna's face, followed quickly by tears. She clutches me, wrapping her arms around my waist as she buries her face in my neck.

"She's alive," she croaks, voice thick with emotion.

My knees weaken beneath me, but Tenna grips me, holding me up. Taking her face in my hands, I kiss her, desperately.

Thank the ancestors…

The thought, pure habit, sours in my mind. I push it away, unwilling to dwell on it just now.

"What happened?" I ask, desperate for answers now that the opportunity has arisen.

"Daet sve ar," Tenna whispers. *The war inside.*

My eyes fill with tears. I rub a hand over my face, nodding.

Of course, she would fight this fight.

I chide myself for not seeing it, for not recognizing it. The war inside was a brutal companion in my younger days. It drove me to the battlefield in the first place. It's what made me such a fierce warrior before I truly knew how to handle myself, because someone with nothing to lose is someone to fear.

Chapter Twenty Two
Odyssey Space Research Station

Olivia

Dull pain radiates through my head, and my throat burns. Darkness coats everything, and slowly, I realize that that's only because my eyes are closed.

I open them to blinding lights, then slam them shut again at the ache in my head.

Were the old religions right?

Is this the bright light of heaven? Or the burning fires of hell?

I try to lift an arm to cover my face, but my muscles are weak. Something tugs at my hand, holding it down. A pinprick of pain in the inner crease of my elbow scares me.

There wouldn't be pain in heaven.

Were they right? Does suicide really damn your soul?

Even out in space, so far from earth and the religions that ruled it?

Forcing myself to face my eternity, I open my eyes. The hospital on Odyssey greets me, and my stomach plummets.

I'm alive...

Tears fill my eyes, and a sob scratches up my throat.

I failed.

A dark shape rises beside me. A hand releases mine, only to reach out, landing gently on my cheek.

"Olivia," Ricardo whispers. "Thank god…"

But any just god would have taken me away from here, away from all the people I could hurt.

"Thank god, you're okay…" he whispers, voice breaking.

But am I?

I'm alive, and all I'll do is hurt people. All I'll do is fail them.

My heart clenches, and my face scrunches up. A hoarse cry bubbles up through my lips.

"Why, Olivia? What was going through your head?"

"No," I say, voice hoarse and rough. "I can't be here. I can't."

Tears pour over my cheeks, and a sob chokes me. Ricardo leans his forehead against mine, staring into my eyes so earnestly.

But I don't deserve that look. I've broken so many lives with my own stupid selfishness. I've destroyed so much.

198

I'm just like my mother…

I slam my eyes shut, blocking out the tenderness in Ricardo's expression, the tenderness I know I don't deserve.

Five little words slip out, half-strangled by the lump in my throat, "I can't be like her."

"You're not like her, Olivia. You didn't kill anyone. You saved people. You are *not* like her."

"But I could've saved more, I could've done more. I was so busy being stupid. I just had to drink and waste my time…" I turn my face away from him. My voice dwindles, becoming small as I say, "And now, they're all dead. Because of me."

"Not because of you. Because of Eva. Because of Robert Mulvaney. Because of all the shitty people that went along with them. Because of my brother…" Ricardo's voice cracks, and he trails off. He shakes his head, moving it against mine.

"You should've let me die," I say, barely audible. "I shouldn't be here."

Ricardo knots his hand in my hair, turning my head to face him. "How many times am I going to have to run down these halls to save you before you realize you're worth saving?"

I open my eyes, staring at him through a sheen of tears. They quickly trickle down my cheeks, leaving his soulful amber eyes crystal clear. My brows furrow before the sincerity I find there, and my lip quivers.

Shaking my head, I deny what he's saying. "I shouldn't be here."

"Yes, you should," Ricardo says, vehemently. "You can have your way on a lot of things, but not on this. You can't leave like that. Whether you believe you deserve to be here or not, whether you believe me when I say that you're *not* like your mom, we need you. You can't leave."

"But I'm not…"

Good enough?

Strong enough?

Smart enough?

"You're needed, Olivia." Ricardo shakes his head softly. "You're *wanted.*"

My insides clench, and a fresh wave of tears bursts forth. Ricardo pulls me up to sitting in my hospital bed, cradling me against his chest. He tucks my head into his neck, and my eyes unleash a torrent of agony.

My arms wrap around him, hands clutching at his back. "I can't do this," I say.

"You can. I'll help. Just please, *please*… talk to me. Next time you start to feel like that, next time you think of…"

A shuddering breath rattles his chest, pulling a sob from me as I see just how deeply I've hurt him. Shock spreads through me.

How can he care about me?

Voice thick with tears, he says, "Just talk to me. Talk to Tenna or Maria. Talk to your counselor. Please…"

And though I hate every bit of myself, though I hate everything I've done, I can't hurt him like this again.

So, I nod, face moving against the soft fabric of his shirt.

But if I can't leave, I'll have to do better.

I'll have to be better.

I can't be like her.

I send a message to my counselor, asking for sessions. I have to do it now, before I lose my nerve.

While Ricardo is still here, showing me exactly why I have to go see her.

***

When they release me from the hospital, they do so only under restrictions. My Link has new programs set to alert

Cait every time I consider suicide, even just in passing, even if my brain just throws it in my face. An injection of antidepressants swirls in my veins, soaking into me. The nurse that administered it smiled softly, clearly hoping it would help me.

But I can't be tempted to take too much of this one, can't store it away for later. I can't get more of it until next month. And they won't let me inject it myself.

I drag my feet down the hall, staring at the floor with my eyes out of focus. Ricardo walks alongside me, but an awkward silence falls over us.

Will it be awkward when I talk to Cait, again?

She'll be so disappointed in me.

A little hiccup of a sob leaps from my lips, and Ricardo puts a gentle hand to the small of my back. "Talk to me?" he asks, soft and sweet.

"It's just been so long since I've seen Cait," I say, knowing he must have met her when I…

"I hadn't been taking my meds, either. They make me sick when I drink."

"So why give up the medicine? Why not give up drinking, instead?" he asks, voice too calm, too comforting.

Too much for the likes of me.

"The pills aren't magic," I answer. "They don't make things go away. They don't undo the shit my mom has done. They don't change the fact that I should've stopped her. They don't bring my dad back or fix my fucked-up life."

"Neither does the alcohol."

"No," I admit, trudging through cold metal halls. "But if I drink enough, I can forget. It takes more and more to feel like it's worth it though. To feel like I'm worth it."

***

"Are you sure you'll be okay?" Ricardo asks, lingering near the door of my room.

The message still glows on his Link, begging him to go to the security offices. But his eyes tense with worry, and a frown pulls his mouth low.

"I can call Maria to sit with you if you want," he offers. "She's been messaging me all day asking how you are, anyway."

God, I hurt her too…

Guilt stabs me in the gut, and I nearly double over. But no tears come, not now. I'm all dried up.

I stare at the messages blinking on the screen of my Link, some from Maria, some from Tenna. Even some from Krona.

But the only ones I've answered are from Cait, finalizing my counseling sessions. Even just the thought of the other messages exhausts me.

Unable to speak, I approach Ricardo and slide my arms around his waist. His arms wrap easily around me, and one hand tucks my head against his chest.

I hurt them all…

I just… didn't think they'd miss me.

Pulling in a deep breath, I say, "I'll be alright alone."

Or as alone as I can be with the Link programmed to tell anything potentially concerning to Cait.

Ricardo's arms tighten around me, and he presses a gentle kiss to the top of my head. The warmth of him seeps into me. My body scrapes out a few tears, sending them to the front lines immediately. They soak into the soft fabric of Ricardo's shirt.

Another message syncs to his Link, letting out a soft beep near my ear. I pull back, wiping the tears away as quickly as I can. I don't want him to see them and shirk his duties for me.

I've already caused enough trouble for him as it is.

"Go," I say. "I'll be fine by myself this time."

He hesitates, staring intently at me. And every second, I hate myself more.

"I promise. I'll still be here when you get done. And I'll have to be alone with what I've done eventually."

Ricardo sighs, "Okay." He rubs a hand over his face, then adds, "If you need anything, just send me a message. I'll be here."

I nod. Reluctantly, I turn away from him, unwilling to hold him back from the promotion I know he's about to get. I slip my shoes off and tuck them under my bed, unwilling to watch him leave.

The door to the hall opens and closes, soft and quiet. Spinning to face it, I stare at the cold metal. In my periphery, I can almost see the ghost of him fighting Lachlan to save me. At my feet, the memory of him holding me as I cried wafts like smoke.

I sit on my bed, running a hand over freshly washed sheets and wishing they still held the memory of us together.

He cares for me. He's done nothing but help me and Daen Tribe.

And I ripped him open.

My hands tremble in my lap, and a sob erupts from me. Tears flow freely once again, dripping from my chin to splatter my sweatpants. I turn on music, letting the sounds of "Bottom of the Deep Blue Sea by MISSIO. 2017" drown out the sound of me crying.

But it doesn't work.

I crank the volume up, but all I hear are my own pitiful cries, my hitching breaths.

My thoughts.

The anguish on Ricardo's face, the messages I can't bring myself to face, the coming executions, the frozen bodies of Regonians awaiting their funerals…

It all swirls in my head, screaming at me.

I turn the volume up louder, despairing at the little beep that interrupts it to tell me I've reached max volume.

It isn't enough.

Springing to my feet, I seek out the little trunk at the foot of my bed. It opens so easily, and there, the whiskey waits for me. I fall to my knees before it, ready to worship at its altar, yet again.

Trembling fingers fumble with the lid.

But I've done this with unsteady hands so many times before.

I bring the bottle to my lips and tip it up, letting a gulp of the fiery liquid burn its way down my throat.

Please, be quick...

Turning, I sit down, leaning against my bed. But another ghost of Ricardo waits to greet me. I see him pausing in the doorway to the bathroom, staring down at me as I drank.

I remember his voice, so fervent. Even now, I can hear him say, "Because I know the types of people who fall to the bottle. I know the types of people who deserve to drown in it." I watch his face soften as he looks me over, then says, "That isn't you."

The ghost of him vanishes into the bathroom, and yet again, I'm alone with my thoughts and the suffocating guilt. Staring down at the bottle in my hand, disgust snakes through me.

What am I doing?

I'm just going to hurt him, again.

Pushing myself to my feet, I carry the bottle to the bathroom.

I can't do this anymore.

I can't.

My hands shake, and tears blur my vision. But the brown glass stands out against the pure white of the sink, clear even through tears.

But what if I have to?

What if I need it?

The executions loom over me, threatening to crush me. My mother's coming death hangs in the back of my mind, waiting to consume me.

I'll need this for that.

I grit my teeth, screaming out, "NO!"

I can't be weak anymore. I can't hurt them again. I can't be so fucking stupid!

Do it. Do it now, before you lose your nerve.

I tip the bottle over the sink, and watch my crutch disappear, drop by fiery drop.

Some crazy part of me wants to lick it out of the sink, just to get a taste, but I shake my head. I turn the water on, rinsing it down before the compulsion becomes too much to resist. The bottle lands with a loud clank when I toss it into the trash.

Ripping my toothbrush and toothpaste from the cabinet, I scrub my mouth out, far too vigorously and for far too long. Leaning over the sink, I spit the foamy mixture out, only to start scrubbing again.

After the third time, I force myself to stop and stow everything away. On the way to my bed, I slam the trunk shut. Though it isn't even dinner time, I tug the blankets down and slide into bed. I pull them up over myself and shut my eyes, hoping sleep will take me quickly.

Chapter Twenty Three
Odyssey Space Research Station

Krona

Morning rolls in, not with a sunrise, not with the setting of four moons, but with a terrible beeping sound from Tenna's alarm and a dull glow emanating from the windows of the space stations in the distance.

Housed in the residential section of the station, we share our quarters with our families. One or two of them, probably Tenna's parents, bustle about beyond the door to our room. They move quietly, and the hiss of a door reverberates through the walls.

But we lay still, wrapped in each other's arms. I pull in a deep breath and kiss Tenna's shoulder. She stares into my eyes and reaches up to smooth a lock of hair back behind my ear. Her lips brush mine, soft and sweet.

"Where shall we even start, today?" she asks, and I feel the weight of everything we must do dragging on her words.

After all, we must contact the Coalition and tell them our decision. The details of the executions need to be settled upon, and we must meet with our Memory Markers to determine a way forward with new tattoos.

But not just yet.

I kiss her neck, then her earlobe. My lips caress sensitive flesh as I say, "We must start with a fresh mind."

I desert her ear for her lips, leaving a trail of kisses in my wake. She slides one leg over me, wrapping it around mine to pull me forward.

I take the invitation eagerly, rolling Tenna onto her back and positioning myself between her legs. My hands roam over her body as our mouths burn together. She teases me, trailing delicate fingers over my spine before sliding them around to my stomach to move lower.

But we haven't time to tarry.

Sliding into her, I move gently, tasting her lips and squeezing her thigh. Our bodies pulse with an ancient rhythm, aching for release, for relief from the worlds beyond this room.

Tenna's nails dig into my back, and she arches in my embrace, pressing perfect breasts against me. She moans, desperate and pleading.

I move deeper within her, pushing myself harder. Her hand thrums between us, and she shatters beneath me with shuddering breaths, calling out my name.

Tumbling down after her, I shake with release as waves of pleasure course through me.

With hands on the back of my neck, Tenna pulls me in for a passionate kiss. Her lips release me, only to whisper, "Hoo kai voo mai."

I answer her the only way I can. "Hoo kai voo mai."

You are my sound.

Chapter Twenty Four
Novay

Rone

I stand anxiously in the center of Facility 15983, the place I've lived and worked all my life. Hundreds of Drennar stand in rows, all at their own slender alonarium pedestal. Cold grey walls wrap around the rectangular room at the heart of this place, but can it be called a heart?

My eyes roam over the Drennar around me, taking in their varied appearances as if for the first time. Some with serpentine bodies coil their tails beneath themselves, supporting their torsos before their pedestals. They wear extra layers, insulating themselves against the cool temperatures of the facility.

A few Drennar wear alonarium membranes, holding water near their gills. Their bare chests and legs glistening with sweat, though I can't comprehend being quite so warm-blooded. Vaguely, I wonder how long they have left before their experiment ends and their lungs are reactivated.

A man nearby with wings similar to mine stands at his podium. No one else here has wings like ours, and my eyes linger on him because of it. Only a harness covers his chest, disappearing beneath his skin. His ears blink, and the podium folds out into screens, showcasing the data from multiple experiments.

His wings are motionless behind him, folded neatly against his bare back.

My own wings flutter restlessly, itching to fly. My mind flits back to my flight this morning and the joy that filled it.

I've never flown just to do it, just to experience it. It's always been for some experiment, aimed at the attainment of very specific information. Soaring above everything, looking down at the whole of what my species has built, I marveled at so many minds working together.

But Reginald's pain hung over me like a pall the whole time, reminding me just how we got all this information in the first place, how we made these advancements.

I cast my gaze around, brows furrowing. On all sides, vacant eyes stare at screens or focus on nothing at all, minds calculating and assimilating new information at breakneck speeds.

But what horrors do they learn from?

On the far side of the room, a woman stands before a scanner, sporting one of the most ambitious experiments thus far. From each shoulder, a new head grows. Both are young, but their growth has been accelerated. Her experiment only began last week, but already, her new heads appear on the verge of reaching maturity.

Multiple brains on one body, processing things at three times the normal rate, processing three times as many experiments, all while consuming only slightly more than the average resources. Accelerated maturation.

Her experiment has many facets, much like my own. We're prototypes. Shiny new things to usher in a new era of information processing.

But I know she doesn't see this the way I do.

She stands before the scanner, motionless save her breathing. She blinks at a perfectly metered rate, just enough to keep her eyes from drying out. Her hands don't fidget at her sides like mine. Her brows don't furrow as mine do.

Because she doesn't question this.

She doesn't have emotions rioting within her.

I turn my gaze to my own podium, a thin grey pedestal, dreading what I'll find and hating my own weakness before this process. Things I've done all my life now seem horrendous. Never before have I struggled to check in on the experiments placed under my care. I always kept a constant stream of incoming data flowing through my mind, even when I stepped away from my pedestal to recharge for the night.

Now, coming in with a clear mind filled with only my thoughts and emotions after an evening with the data stream metered down to monitor only a few things, hoping for just a little peace, my palms sweat. My heart races, and my breathing hitches.

Swallowing, I issue the command and sync to my pedestal. My ears blink once to signal the successful connection. The evening's events on Gordeky come rushing into my mind, and again, I find myself rooting for a child on a distant planet, a girl named Kiluna. I hope for her survival, biased in this experiment in a way I never was before.

Security footage shows her grandmother smoothing hair out of her face and administering to wounds too severe for a child to suffer through.

And my heart clenches.

Even as my mind processes the data, measuring every beat of their hearts, every blink, every movement and word, my chest collapses. The corners of my eyes prick, and tears slide over my cheeks. A breath hitches in my throat.

I glance around at the Drennar around me. My breath comes fast, and dread fills me as they turn toward me.

Those nearest me step away from their podiums, approaching. Heat blooms over my skin as fans of light erupt from their eyes, sweeping over me. They measure me, analyzing every breath, every shake of my shoulders, every rustle of feathered wings. They weigh the air that leaves me, check its temperature, check how quickly my synapses fire.

My frown deepens, and my cheeks burn. I falter before them, dropping my gaze, and I know they measure the speed at which my head falls, the surface temperature of the skin of my face to compare it with that of the rest of me, the shift of every hair on my head.

On the screen before me, the experiment set up by my forebears plays out. Parents weep near the unconscious girl, laid out in her bed.

My heart lurches, skipping a few beats in a painful downward spiral. More fans of light sweep over me, and I drop to the ground, crouching on the balls of my feet. I drop my head onto my knees, hugging them and curling into a ball with one hand sprawled over the top of my head.

Tears leak from me, soaking into the fabric that covers my knees.

Still, they analyze me, more and more Drennar stepping up to do their own calculations. Vivid blue light flickers on the floor around me as their fans overlap. Shadows convulse as they scan me from the other side of pedestals.

I ache to disappear, to run from them.

But they'd only follow. And everyone I pass would join in.

Get a grip on yourself.

This experiment will not rule you.

But my petulant chiding does no good.

They won't stop until you return to normal.

The hope this offers, the lifeline, is too promising to ignore. So, I imagine the girl on Gordeky smiling a few days before her attack. I picture Reginald laughing beside me. I replay moments from Olivia's childhood, from Krona and Tenna's life before we showed the Humans how to find them.

218

And a smile tugs at the corners of my lips, trying to pull me to my feet.

I wipe my eyes, urging them to stop producing tears. Pulling in a slew of deep breaths, I marvel at their ability to steady me. Another strange little thing the Humans always talked about, but which we dismissed as nonsense.

Slowly, I rise to my feet and stare down at my pedestal. I break the scene before me down into numbers, as I've always been taught to do. The coldness of it feels wrong, but it keeps my eyes dry long enough for the others to return to their normal work.

I maintain my objective analysis, trying to keep from thinking about the way their ears blink, syncing my breakdown so that every Drennar in existence can analyze their findings.

My own ears blink as I receive all their transmissions.

And for the first time in my life, I don't open the messages, don't immediately assimilate their data into my own views of myself.

I'll process these later.

When I'm alone.

A small part of me rebels at the thought of hoarding my reaction to their information, stealing that knowledge from them. I tell myself that I'll record the entire process.

But I shudder at the thought of it, and I know I won't do it.

Chapter Twenty Five
Odyssey Space Research Station

Ricardo

Olivia laces her fingers through mine as we walk through long metal halls. We wind through the station, moving slowly. She barely looks up.

Does she dread seeing the hospital again?

I do.

Visions of her lying helpless and unconscious in that bed, face drawn and pale from her suicide attempt, haunt me. They dog my steps, promising to paint themselves over every bed in the hospital.

I squeeze Olivia's hand, reassuring myself that she's here, she's alive. She surprises me, looking up into my eyes. The furrow of her brows, the crease between them reminds me that she feels guilty for troubling me.

"I'm glad you asked me to walk you to see Cait," I say. "I wanted to spend some time with you."

And though I say it to comfort her, it certainly isn't a lie.

A thin sheen of tears shines in her eyes, and for a moment, I wonder if I've said something wrong. But only for a moment.

She needs to know she's wanted here.

At the door to the hospital, I pull in a fortifying breath. I keep my eyes away from the beds as best I can.

Olivia squeezes my hand, and now, it's my turn to look at her. Beautiful hazel eyes stare into mine, tight with concern and sadness.

"I can find my way from here," she says, lighter than I expect, maybe even a bit teasing. But sincerity finds her once again as she says, "Thank you."

Nodding, I say, "No problem."

She releases my hand, leaving me cold in the absence of her touch. "I'll see you at lunch," she says, walking toward an office in the back.

An office I visited for my own sake just yesterday morning.

Cait comes to the door, anticipating her. She smiles, kind and welcoming. She even waves at me before ushering Olivia into the warmth of her office.

Chapter Twenty Six
Odyssey Space Research Station

Olivia

Cait sits across from me, smiling gently. Her makeup fights to conceal dark circles beneath her warm eyes, and I wonder how much of that battle has been lost on my account.

A twinge of guilt twists in my gut, and I drop my gaze. I stare at my hands, watching myself pick at a little burr on the side of one nail.

But the trembling of my fingers makes the burr impossible to catch.

"How was your morning?" Cait begins, easing into things.

My brittle nerves crack under the pressure of knowing how obvious I am, how clear it is to everyone that I'm a broken, fragile thing.

Words desert me.

All I can manage is a shrug.

I don't tell her that I woke up crying. Or that I cried myself to sleep. Or that Ricardo held me as I sobbed.

Or that I see thousands of dead Regonians every time I close my eyes.

"When was your last drink?" Cait asks.

Shame burns me, coloring my cheeks. I drop my head forward, trying to hide my face from her.

"Last night," I whisper, forcing myself to own up to this. "I felt so shitty though, I only had one drink. I poured the rest down the drain."

"So then, why did you drink last night?"

Tears prick at the corners of my eyes, and my skin burns. I hold my tongue, dreading the pity and anger I'm sure will radiate from her eyes.

We sit in silence, Cait apparently content to wait for an answer.

And I cave.

"I felt so guilty..." I drop my head into my hands, and the tears pour out. "I didn't think it would hurt anyone if I died. I didn't think anyone would care."

A blurry flash of Ricardo kneeling over me in Sparrow stabs my heart, and fresh sobs wrack my body.

"Of course, people care. There are a great many people who care about you," Cait gentles.

"Yeah, and I hurt them," I splutter. Finally, I look up, staring into warm brown eyes. "I was too blind to see what I was doing, and people got hurt."

Which basically sums up my entire fucking life.

My heart clenches painfully, and I falter before Cait's steady gaze.

Staring at my hands through a shimmer of tears, I say, "Just like with the Regonians."

Chapter Twenty Seven
Novay

Reginald

Rone laughs, musical and sweet. Her eyes sparkle as she relays the details of a Human sitcom she watched this afternoon, some show called Friends. Our knees, drawn up onto my bed, almost touch. A fever runs through my veins, aching for me to scoot closer to her, for me to kiss her.

But then, she'd stop laughing.

So, I listen as she tells me about the characters in the show, grateful that if we had to be apart for testing today, she at least had an enjoyable afternoon. The day's equations still buzz in my head, whispering promises of advancements for all the Human tech that I'll never be able to improve.

Rone says something about an umbrella opening suddenly and smacking a woman in a wedding dress in the show, and though I don't understand the reference, she laughs hysterically. A smile spreads itself over my face.

"I'm sorry to ramble," she says. "It was just so good. I wish you could've been watching with me."

"No need to apologize. I wish I'd been there too," I say. And even though I love the days where I actually get to learn something rather than be tortured with the devastation of humanity and my family, I really do wish I'd been with Rone.

I stare into her eyes, watching the vivid blue shift within the green as whatever tech lurks within her irises calibrates. But it's so much a part of her that I don't often think of it as tech.

It's just her.

A soft blush spreads over her pale grey skin, and her lids fall closed, fanning thick lashes over her cheeks. She peeks up at me, peering through those dark lashes. "What is it?" she asks.

I tip my head to the side and say, "You're beautiful."

Her chest rises with a deep breath.

Now that it won't steal her laughter away, I lean in, brushing my lips over hers. A million butterflies erupt in my stomach, and my heart hammers against my ribs. My hands ache to reach out, and my entire body comes alive.

But god, what if I mess up?

I'm so out of practice.

Rone puts a hand to the side of my neck, igniting my skin at her touch. The world burns around me, stealing the breath from my lungs.

Her lips part, and I take the invitation. Our tongues dance, and the gravity between us becomes too much. I reach out, sliding my hands up into her hair and pulling her to me.

She trails her hand down to my chest, and her lips forsake mine, moving lower. A deep, guttural sound escapes me as she kisses the delicate skin of my neck.

My hands wander, dipping to her waist. I grip her hip, hesitant to move any further despite the ache within me. My heart pounds, and my breath comes in short gasps as I seek Rone's lips, once more. She meets me with renewed fervor, eager to let our mouths resume their dance.

With trembling fingers, I push the hem of her shirt up to her waist, tracing nonsensical patterns on her bare flesh, and she shivers, pulling in a deep breath. Her wings rustle, fluttering dark feathers against my pillows.

One of her hands deserts my chest, reaching back over her shoulders to undo the knot that secures her shirt between her wings. The fabric falls away in one fluttering motion, and my heart lodges in my throat.

My gaze roams over her, tracing the taut peaks of her breasts, lingering at the hollows of her collarbones. Our lips meet once more, and I lift one tremulous hand, letting my fingers graze the skin of her ribs. Gently, I cup her breast, and every muscle in my body aches with the sweetest tension I've ever known.

Rone moans softly against my lips, spurring me on. Letting my thumb play, I lean into her. A ravenous hunger guides me, pushing me to taste her. I kiss her neck, her collarbone, her shoulder.

She gasps, digging her nails into my back. The fabric of my shirt bunches in her grasp, and she quickly pulls it up and over my head.

Questing hands trace the outlines of my shoulder blades, the curve of my spine. I shiver at her touch, and she pushes me onto my back. Straddling me, she moves against me as our lips melt together.

Grasping her buttocks, I pull her down against me, relishing the feel of her. Tight peaks brush my chest, drawing my senses into a frenzy. Sliding my hands down under the skin-tight fabric of her pants, I squeeze her backside, and she whimpers against my lips.

In one swift motion, I push her pants down over her hips. She kicks the unwanted clothing away, dappling my neck with gentle kisses all the while. When she straddles me again, my hands drift up her thighs, relishing her ragged breathing.

I trace her hip, then let my fingers play on the sensitive flesh near her belly button.

But her decided lack of a belly button startles me. Our previous conversation on Drennar reproduction and all Rone's modifications screams back into my mind. And my nerves almost get the better of me.

But she nibbles softly at my ear, dredging up a moan from the depths of my soul.

Sliding my hand lower, I test the waters.

Oh...

Oh. This is good. This is very good.

I stifle a chuckle at myself and my fears. What was I expecting, after all? A million images of aliens in old Earth movies come to mind, packed to the brim with gore and terrifying things, tentacles and teeth where they shouldn't be.

But as I dip deeper into Rone, nothing feels alien.

She moans, nuzzling her face into my neck. Her hand finds its way down, rubbing vigorously through the soft fabric of my pants. I arch my back, tensing beneath her. All the worlds narrow to this moment as Rone pushes my pants down, freeing me from their restraints.

Our lips meet, and I move my fingers over her, pushing her toward frenzy. She gasps, and her thighs shake. But still, my hand moves faster.

She arches her back, showing me the full glory of her body as my fingers move deftly within her. Her wings sprawl out behind her, black feathers consuming the room. When I withdraw my hand, she sits back, taking me in.

My entire body ignites. The air rushes from me in a deep, soul-wrenching moan. She moves, rolling her hips, and lightning arcs across my skin.

I sit up, ravaging her neck, grasping her hips. Pulling her down, sinking deeper into her, I bite her bottom lip. Desperate and aching, hungry and burning alive, I wrap one arm around her waist, pulling her down hard.

Slipping my other hand between us, I work her to a fever pitch. She convulses, falling apart in my arms. I lift her up, only to bring her down over myself again, plunging deep.

And stars explode across my vision as I shatter.

***

Tangled in each other's arms, we lay in my bed drifting in and out of a warm half-sleep. My fingers move idly over Rone's upper arm, and she grazes my chest with her lips.

A gentle hiss at the other end of my room draws my attention. Opening my eyes, I see another Drennar standing in the doorway. I sit bolt upright, grabbing up my blanket to drape it over us. An odd pang of familiarity sweeps through me at the sight of him. Panic swells within me, kicking my heart up to an awful pace.

What will they do to Rone for this?

How did I not think of that before?

The Drennar in the doorway stares on, wings motionless behind him, even as Rone sits up beside me, holding the blanket up to her chest.

Twin fans of blue light emanate from his eyes, sweeping over us. Not a single muscle twitches in his face. The little blue lights in the tips of his ears blink, transmitting the information he's just gathered.

He crosses all four arms behind his back, staring impassively down at us. Gills flutter on his neck behind thin membranes of water, and the blue circles of light within his dark eyes shine.

Rone slides her hand into mine, squeezing tight. But it offers me little comfort.

The tips of his ears blink three times, brilliant blue dazzling next to his dark grey skin, and finally, he opens his mouth to speak.

"Come with me."

Beside me, Rone whispers, "Lustran, I promise, you don't understand."

He stares at us, impassionate, and repeats, "Come with me."

A sick feeling writhes in my gut as we rise from the bed.

Chapter Twenty Eight
Odyssey Space Research Station

Olivia

Reeling from the day, I sit in Cait's office, tucked in the back of the hospital. Though she rearranged her schedule to fit mine, squeezing me in for another session before I leave to take Tenna and Krona to Termana, I can barely bring myself to speak.

My mother's death sentence lingers in my mind.

"How are you feeling?" Cait asks, pushing me to talk.

And isn't that her job?

Isn't that why I'm here?

To talk?

Regardless, it takes me several moments to speak, stepping carefully to the side of my real thoughts and avoiding her question, "They demanded my mom's death."

"Did you expect something different?" Cait asks.

No...

I sit silently, picking at the hem of my shirt. Cait doesn't speak, letting me stew, and tension builds within me.

"I don't know…" I hedge. "They *are* warriors. I guess I'm surprised they didn't want more people dead." My tone sours, misplacing my anger, my guilt. I cringe, recognizing what I'm doing and hating that I'm doing it anyway.

"Had the Coalition decided the punishment without letting them speak, what do you think they would have chosen?"

"Death." I sigh, staring down at my hands.

"Yet, you seem surprised."

"I guess I just… didn't think about that part of it. I didn't think about how it would end. I just knew she had to be stopped." Tears prick at my eyes as guilt gnaws at me, and I know Cait must guess my feelings. Nothing slips past her.

We sit in silence, and I know she's waiting me out. But I can't bring myself to speak, can't force words past the lump in my throat.

Apparently guessing as much, she says, "Just like you, Tenna did what she had to do, but she said she feels terrible that it's hurting you."

Finally, I look up, meeting Cait's eyes. "Did she ask about me? Did you talk to her about me?" My stomach plummets as betrayal wraps fiery hands around my heart.

"No, no. We did have a rather interesting conversation though. Did you know Daen Tribe has a position similar to what I do?" Cait says, offering me a blissful moment of distraction.

"They call them Memory Keepers," she continues. "They're marked with a single blue ring on their chest. They never tell anyone what's told them in confidence, and if they break their oath, their tongue is removed, which, by the way, is the worst punishment they can face."

I tip my head, considering this. Curiosity gets the better of me, pulling me up from my slumped posture, though only slightly.

"They're the only members of Daen Tribe to be tattooed after death," Cait continues. "Two black rings outline the blue ring, one on the inside and one on the outside, because the confessions they heard die with them."

I swallow, but the tension within me eases.

"Needless to say, Tenna perfectly understands my oath. She didn't ask a single question. Not one. But she knows you're hurting." Cait's eyes soften. "Though she knows she did what she had to do, she's sorry that it's hurting you."

My throat constricts, and tears return. I hunch forward, digging elbows into my knees and burying my face in my hands.

Cait falls silent, and my sobs are the only sounds in the room.

"Whether directed at you or at Tenna, what do you think your anger means?" Cait asks.

Eventually, choking on my own defensiveness, I dare, "You tell me."

Silence falls yet again, but this time, I hold my ground.

Cait gives in, saying, "I think, sometimes, it's easier to be angry, easier to hide, than it is to deal with grief or guilt. The trouble is, hiding just means that you can't heal."

Chapter Twenty Nine
Odyssey Space Research Station

Tenna

Krona wraps his hand around mine as we venture to the hangar. My heart lurches in my chest, but I keep my pace even. I need my people to see me going toward this meeting confidently, not panicking and running full speed ahead.

But I need to see Olivia.

I need to know she's alive.

And I'm not the only one. Krona's grip tightens with each step. His battle with the war inside as a young man haunts him, striking a fierce dilemma within him.

Without it, he would've worked in the fields as his parents and grandparents did. The war inside pushed him to the battle fields, seeking death in one form or another.

That led him here.

But it nearly killed him before we ever met.

How many times have I talked him down from this exact turmoil? And yet, I didn't even recognize the signs in Olivia.

The metal halls drag on for an eternity, spreading out before us as guilt settles in my gut. It weighs me down, making the walk to the hangar feel even longer.

249

When we finally reach the airlock, when we finally see her, gaunt and staring at the floor, Krona and I rush forward. We throw our arms around her, pulling her into a hug.

She weeps in our arms, and I rest my forehead against Krona's, crying in earnest.

***

On Termana, Olivia and Ricardo lead us from the hangar to the elevators. We walk down a single metal hallway, passing windows as we go. Beyond, a series of metal boxes perch on the landscape, dotted with windows and doors. Some stack high above the ground.

Soft shades of cerulean and forest green try to make the place look natural. Planters hang in most windows, and tiny, patches of grass perch in front of every metal home or building as far as the eye can see in an attempt to bring their old world with them.

But I look up, peering past the lights Olivia once told me mimic the sunlight of Earth. Just beyond them, I see the metal shell that encases the Human world, and pity fills me.

Their only refuge, their only home, has been invaded by the Drennar, just as our home was invaded by some of the Humans. They know the loss of abduction.

And I'm counting on that.

Twining my fingers with Krona's, I lift my chin higher, preparing myself for what's to come. I try desperately to put away the rage that simmers within me, despite the revenge I've already taken.

Efsi's killer died on the battlefield, died by my hand if not by the Vyrto bone I carved into an axe before taking the throne.

But even his death didn't ease the violent fury within, didn't account for the even greater tragedy. And my people still await justice.

Olivia stops in front of an unassuming metal door. It blends in with the steel blue of the walls so well that had Olivia not stopped, I would have kept on walking. But she raps on the door with her fist, pulling a voice from the void beyond.

"Come in."

So, we do.

Krona and I duck through the door after our friends enter the conference room. Dr. Sullivan sits at a table with the remaining four members of the Survival Coalition and the Honorable Judge Supreme Martine.

Soldiers stand in each corner with hands clasped behind their backs. Guns hang at their sides, as do lightning sticks. My heart skips a beat, and my eyes narrow.

Krona's grip on my hand tightens, and I know he's seen them too. My hand goes to my side, fumbling uselessly where my blade should be. But I know I won't need it against these frail humans if it comes to that.

Dr. Sullivan rises to his feet, turning to usher us into the room. He tracks our gazes and hurries to reassure us. "Any Guard charged with protecting the Coalition carries their weapons openly. That's just standard procedure. Our leaders are not quite so well-versed in combat as yourselves. They require Guards."

I raise one eyebrow, assimilating the knowledge that the Human leaders can't defend themselves, even against other Humans. Then, I process the knowledge that they might need protection from their own people.

Given all the atrocities some of their leaders have committed in the scraps of Human history that I've learned and in the time that I've been here, that isn't quite as surprising as it should be.

I skim the Humans collected before me, raking my eyes over their soft frames. Either too petite to absorb a single blow or too large to escape one, not a one of them would survive a battle of any sort.

I nod, taking a step toward two chairs obviously meant for us. They dwarf every other chair in the room. Relief floods through me at the prospect of sitting on furniture large enough to accommodate me.

Krona sits to my left with Ricardo on his other side. Olivia sits to my right. Her hands tremble in her lap, and I reach over, wrapping my free hand around hers.

After introductions are made, Patricia McDonough, Minister of Education, reads off an exceedingly long and dull recitation of the alliance terms put forth at the tribunal.

Her rich brown eyes shine, radiating sympathy every time her gaze meets mine or Krona's. That kindness suits her soft, delicate features.

"We have spoken with certain civilians on Odyssey Station as to their demands for the repairs of their home and conversion of the labs into an ethical place of work," she says.

Shadows play in the hollows of her collarbones as she dips her head to stare at the papers before her, darkening her blue-black skin even further. "Those terms have been agreed upon, and we are already working to complete them."

Glancing back up from her notes, she meets Krona's gaze, then mine. As the natural born ruler, she should have met my gaze first.

Beneath the table, Krona squeezes my hand, but I already know to let it slide. She doesn't know our customs, doesn't know the offense. In her youth, my mother would have had McDonough's head on a pike.

But I am not my mother.

I gently squeeze Krona's hand to let him know that I mean the woman no harm.

"The terms that you put forth at the tribunal have already been agreed to. We shall see the perpetrators executed for their crimes," McDonough's gaze strays to Olivia, then Ricardo as the words leave her lips, brows drawing together. "Your people will be given safe passage home. All experiments have already been reversed."

Krona and I incline our heads, acknowledging the efforts these Humans have already gone to in an attempt to repair the atrocities committed against us.

Sitting forward in her chair, Lisa Chong, Minister of Agriculture, says, "We need only an answer from you as to whether you accept the alliance. It will not change our agreement to your previous terms. We understand that you were brought into this war without your consent, and we know that we have no right to expect participation. But we are hopeful."

I glance at Krona, finding strength and reassurance in his eyes.

Then, I face the Human leaders and say, "We were brought into this war without our consent, that is true. But it may well become our war if the Drennar come for us as they have come for you. We have no way of knowing how long they've been watching us. We don't know why. We don't know what they plan to do in the future."

"If given the choice between waiting for an attack, exhausting ourselves with wondering, or going to battle, we will take matters into our own hands," I say. "We accept your proposal of an alliance, provided that we retain autonomy and reign over our own forces. Our people will *not* be yours to command."

The air pressure in the room shifts as several people let out breaths.

"We do have two additional requests, though," I add.

The Coalition members glance at each other, faces tense. Lisa Chong fiddles with the edge of a paper, further ruffling the unorganized stack.

"The needles they made from our bones must be returned to us."

A sick feeling slides through me as I recall the first time I saw one, back when Dr. Antar used one to steal my blood. Even then, I knew it shouldn't dive so deep into my flesh. Our Memory Markers use bone needles, but they never drive them in so far.

They'll have their hands full with the Marks of the Awakening. And they certainly won't have time to carve new needles from the bones of the Memory Marker that perished.

Not that they could ever make enough for so many Marks from one person.

Stunned, the Coalition members stare at me, but I'll not explain our customs here and now. This is not the time.

"Okay," Johnathan Croon, Minister of Human Affairs, answers. A strand of silver hair hangs loose by his ear, just touching his jaw. He smooths it back quickly. "And your other request?"

My stomach flips, and my heart accelerates. "The guilty must die as their victims did." I don't speak of those killed in the field of battle on Termana, though my heart begs me to demand a grisly death for those who soaked our fields in blood.

Messages flicker on their Links, glowing in various colors. They glance at each other over and again.

Finally, Terrence Ulric, Minister of Treasury and Commerce, speaks. "It *would* be rather cost effective as the… beds… on Washington Station have yet to be completely dismantled. And our traditional method of execution would never accommodate so many." He glances at the others, jowls shaking as he does so, then adds, "We agree to your requests."

Sitting forward in his chair, Johnathan Croon smiles. "I'm so glad to have that behind us so we can move forward. I do have one last question, though. The Drennar are quite a… formidable foe. Do you have any allies that we might call on?"

Chapter Thirty
Novay

Reginald

Rone and I follow the Drennar she called Lustran down the hall. His body suit shines in the bright light that seems to radiate from everywhere and nowhere at once. By contrast, Rone's soft shirt absorbs the light, begging for me to touch it, to reach inside it for the light it holds.

My heart hammers in my chest though. Because reaching under that fabric may have doomed me, may have doomed Rone.

What have I done?

How many times will I do what I think is right only to mess up my own life and the lives of those I care about?

I shake my head, trying not to berate myself for the mess Eva made of her life. Or the trauma she subjected Olivia to, neglecting her for years in my absence.

Those choices weren't mine. I can't beat myself up for them.

But I know I will.

Just as I know I will beat myself up over whatever comes of the pulsing of my heart as Rone and I joined together in my bed and the too-quick beats of Lustran's feet on the floor, leading us to certain doom.

Fear draws my brows together and dries my mouth out. I swallow painfully, loudly.

A single glance finds Rone walking with her chin held aloft, confident despite the circumstances. But what does she know that I don't?

So much.

She knows so much *more than I do.*

My blood freezes as I wonder for the first time if I've been duped, if this was just another experiment. Her smile flashes in my memory, and the sweet melody of her laughter flutters through my mind, trying so hard to reassure me. Her tears fall on my skin, soak into my shirt in my head, so convincing.

Could she have pretended?

Did she fool me?

But as we round a steel-blue corner, she wraps her hand around mine. She laces our fingers together and gives my hand a squeeze.

I glance at her again, and she smiles. She actually smiles. Despite everything, despite the fact that we were caught.

Surely, this can't be good.

But she whispers to me, conspiratorially, "It'll be fine."

Lustran stops in front of a blank wall, insignificant and so much like every other wall here. His ears blink, and the wall folds in on itself to allow us passage.

Beyond the door, many Drennar sit in white chairs with eyes glazed over. All have their own modifications, some of which I've never seen before. My brain struggles to put the pieces together, staring at them in awe and terror. A series of blinks on Lustran's ear tips immediately spurs a mirroring series on all their ears.

They turn to face us in unison, bodies perfectly synchronized. Chills run down my spine as I stare on, terrified of the hive before me and the collective power of their minds.

If I've outlived my usefulness, if they think I've corrupted Rone in some way...

What will they do to me?

Would my destruction be swift and painless for the sake of efficiency?

Or merciless and agonizing as an experiment of some sort?

My free hand trembles. I curl it into a fist, attempting to hold it still, to no avail. If they knew anything about emotion,

I'd worry that they might misinterpret it as anger, some primitive rage at having been disturbed in an act they could never truly understand.

"Rone," Lustran says, voice a cool monotone. It chills me worse than a furious shout ever could. "I do not understand the motivations behind your actions. Your behavior is an anomaly that I would like to know more about. Even now, you entwine yourself with this lower being. Could you explain?"

For the first time in a long time, they speak in their own language, perhaps wishing to impede my ability to participate in the conversation. The translator allows enough of a delay to hold my tongue.

"This isn't something you can understand in your current state," Rone says, easily, calmly.

I gape at her.

"Do we lack the proper modifications?" a seated Drennar asks. Silver blades stick out from her scalp, glimmering in the ambient light.

What experiment could those have been for?

"You do. We, Drennar, lack the fundamental biology to understand," Rone says. Her tone never wavers, never betrays even a hint of the emotion I've heard within it recently. "It is not possible to fully understand Humans without emotion."

The Drennar before us sit silently, processing the concept of never understanding something. Silence rings loudly, and I look at them, really look.

Gills adorn several necks. Many have clear sections of skull, allowing complete visibility. Streaks of blue light shoot through teal brain matter, spiraling through the folds. Hoses and various plugs rest within arms and chests.

One even has a strange, many-screened device sticking out of one eye socket, and another surprisingly meek creature looks like a fairy come to life.

With all their modifications, how far will they push themselves to understand? How deeply does it trouble them to not understand something?

At long last, their ear tips blink. All around the massive room, little flashes of light grapple for my attention, drowning me in a sea of unanswered questions.

My heart beats frantically, hammering my lungs and breaking my breath into shattered, staccato pulses.

The messages stop, and the blinking fades.

Lustran focuses his attention on Rone and says, "Some of those present wish to have the proper modifications done to allow understanding, myself included. The new experiment will begin tomorrow. Your assistance may be required for any adjustment period."

My ears perk up at one of the words, recognizing it before the translator ever comes across it, and my stomach drops. Ice flows through my veins, but I'm allowed no time to process it.

"I readily agree," Rone answers.

Turning to me, Lustran shifts seamlessly into my language, saying, "Once I have been modified, I wish to speak with you further so that I might understand you."

A chill skitters over my spine, but I nod my acquiescence.

"Are all the modifications necessary, or simply emotion?" he asks.

"What?" I ask, brows creasing my forehead. "What do you mean, 'all the modifications?'"

"Sex organs and drives. Are those necessary aspects of understanding humanity?"

I nearly choke on the question. For half a breath, I analyze humanity and the massive impact sex has had on the shaping of our species.

Could we be understood with no real understanding of that drive?

"I think they may be," I finally answer, though I have no idea what consequences will come of *this* answer.

"But you are uncertain?" Lustran asks. Fans of blue light erupt from his eyes, startling me as they sweep over my body.

"Wars have been waged over desires throughout our history, but there are a few among us that feel no desire for romantic entanglements."

"They are anomalies?" the blade-scalped Drennar asks, grasping for some sort of understanding.

My brows come together, put off by her phrasing, but I stammer, "I suppose so, yes."

Another flurry of messages erupts over the tips of their ears. As soon as it stops, Lustran says, "The modifications will be done immediately. A small group will receive only emotion to replicate the anomalies."

Rone squeezes my hand gently, pulling my attention from the hive of cold, indestructible aliens before me. She smiles, and in my periphery, a cacophony of light erupts over the others' ears.

How many are here? Thirty? Forty?

How many of them will have emotion?

Will they all regret their prior experiments as she seems to? If they do, what does that mean for humanity?

I ache to ask Rone if this was her plan, if she knew this would happen.

Is that why she wanted to be with me? Or does she actually have feelings for me?

My mind whirls with questions, and my stomach churns, but I can't say a word. Not here. In a species driven only toward understanding, her manipulating them for my sake would surely be treason.

She escorts me back to my room, smiling all the way. Our hands never part. Once back within relative safety, once my wall hisses back into place, I turn to her, ready to ask a million questions.

But they all die on my lips, cowed by the fear of losing the only person I have left.

My mouth hangs, lips parted with the start of a question, so I say the first thing that comes to mind, drifting back to the conversation between Rone and Lustran. "The word Regonia…"

She waits patiently, but I can't figure out how to ask my question.

"The race of people that Eva…" I close my eyes, gritting my teeth against her travesties. "They call themselves Regonians. Why?"

"They refer to themselves in terms of their planet, but they don't know the actual meaning of the word." Rone's eyes fall to the floor. "It was erased from their vocabulary when they were put on those planets."

My heart freezes, skidding to a cold stop within my chest.

And though I know I could have my translator confirm it, this needs to be spoken with a real voice, a voice with emotion.

Maybe that will soften the blow.

So, I ask, "Does it mean what I think it means?"

She meets my gaze with deep lines etched into her skin. A sigh lifts her shoulders, and she whispers, "Regonia means... experiment."

Chapter Thirty One
SCCS Sparrow

Olivia

Ricardo chooses the music as we fly back to Odyssey. "No Glory in the West by Orville Peck. 2020" eases out of the speakers throughout Sparrow on slow guitar strokes and a deep voice.

He must really like this song to have paid for it.

As we leave the hangar and venture into the stars, it soothes my soul, just a touch. But the ache of saying goodbye to Tenna and Krona still tugs the corners of my lips downward.

I stare out at the vast expanse of space before me, trying to shake the memory of my last time here in Sparrow, trying to shake the pain in Tenna's and Krona's embrace this morning.

I hurt them, too.

And now they know how weak I am.

What will Daen tribe think of me?

A tear hovers on the edge of my lashes, but I brush it away. I dry the back of my hand on my pants to keep the tear from rolling off my hand onto a control panel.

Ricardo clears his throat, and I brace myself. I half expect him to tell me how much he hates what I did, for him to make sure I know just how shitty it was.

I steal a glance at him, but he doesn't meet my gaze. He stares off through Sparrow's window, eyes wide with wonder.

He may not have even seen my stupid little tear. He might have just been clearing his throat because he needed to.

"What do you think Regonia is like?" he asks.

I take a moment to reorganize myself, shifting to this unexpected topic. We drift closer to Odyssey Station, and it obscures more and more of the heavens.

"I don't know. Tenna didn't remember anything, so she couldn't tell me much." My head fills with the agony my mother put her through, and another tear threatens to fall. Desperate for a distraction, aching to give my mind something new to play with, I ask, "Did Krona tell you anything?"

Ricardo nods in my periphery.

"Can you tell me about it?"

Again, I steal a glance. A soft smile decorates his handsome face, and a single, curly strand of hair dangles loose at his temple.

He looks nothing like the man I woke up to in the hospital, grief-stricken and broken by my fuck up. And though I know the pain is still there, it makes me wonder.

Maybe I didn't break him completely.

Refocusing my attention, I steer us toward the hangar on Odyssey. As I set us down, Ricardo tells me that Regonia has four moons. The turntable rotates beneath us as his tone turns wistful, telling me how the Regonians use the moons' positions on any given night to tell where they're at in their year.

It sounds so much nicer than our calendars and clocks. Most people on Termana never even see the stars beyond the metal shell. Not everyone sneaks up freight elevators and into the shell as a kid like I did.

All they see is the same gentle slope of the little rock we've claimed for our species, the metal boxes they all live in.

"Do they have mountains?" I ask, hopeful. "Or an ocean?"

A soft sigh eases past Ricardo's lips, drawing out the word as he says, "Both. The ocean spreads over the entire horizon if you climb up the mountains Taron Tribe lives on."

He unfastens his harness but doesn't rise. So, I hold the hangar bay open with a thought, content to stare out at the stars with him for a while.

***

My alarm wakes me bright and early, and for the first time in weeks, it doesn't irritate a hangover or withdrawals. My head doesn't pulse with the agony of over- or underindulgence.

But all the things I want to hide from are there, lurking in the shadows, clearer and more present without the warm, velvety fog of alcohol.

My mother leers at me from a dark corner of my mind. Medical equipment shines in her hands. My father languishes in another empty sector of my thoughts, far beyond my reach. And everywhere, I see the dead Regonians, shaking with the currents of their death.

Unable to bear the sight, I open my eyes.

Ricardo's sleeping face rests mere centimeters from mine. Countless strands of dark, bushy curls sprawl over the pillow behind him. A few drape over his forehead. I let my eyes trace them for a moment, but I don't reach for him for fear of waking him.

His t-shirt collar twists oddly, stretched down toward the bed from when he rolled to face me earlier. Our hands lay between us, tangled and laced together. I smile, recalling the groggy way he searched for my hand, pawing at my wrist and feeling his way up to my palm.

For a moment, I consider staying here, whiling away the morning just staring at him.

The video call with the Coalition isn't until 9:00...

But there are other things I wanted to do first, things I need to check. The Coalition's commands of maintaining Atlantis until I can train others in its use echo through my head, kicking me for trying to abandon them all without even thinking of that. Guilt churns within me, burning me from the inside out.

Reluctantly, I slide my hand from Ricardo's, disentangling our fingers. Every second of pulling away from him hurts.

But I roll out of bed and seek my laptop. I just don't stay away for long, dropping back into bed as soon as I have it. I push my pillow up against the wall and settle in.

Nestling closer, Ricardo slides his arm over my lap, gripping my hip and nuzzling his face into my side. Soft sleep sounds whisper over his lips, and heat rushes through me. Our first and only night together flashes through my mind, reminding me just how skilled his hands are, just how passionate he can be.

But we haven't come close since.

I stare down at him, relishing the feel of his hand on my hip and his hair tickling my waist where my shirt slid up. For a single heartbeat, I consider waking him up, kissing his lips.

But a flash of guilt spikes through me.

I open my laptop, resting it on my legs. Ricardo's arm makes it difficult to type, but I refuse to move him away. So, I resort to thinking my commands.

The screen flashes symbols and letters, showing me layers of encryption. I enter my password a few times, working my way deep into Atlantis. Then, I check the perimeter.

Several attempts have been made to enter Termana or a Station, though they ceased after the first two days.

And the Drennar have been blocked, so far.

How many did they have nearby?

The only way they'd know we didn't accidentally blow ourselves out of the sky is if they were close enough to see us.

I keep sifting, looking past communications sent within our net, and find a video message sent from a Drennar. My face scrunches up at the prospect.

Since when do they try to reach us so… directly?

After a scan for nearby crafts and another for any current attempts to break through Atlantis, I disconnect from the universal net and reach into my nightstand. An old device, forgotten and long-since replaced, waits for me.

Equipped with its own net, it operates outside Atlantis, separate from it. I find and scan the message thoroughly, checking for anything malicious, then download that message directly to the device. I quickly disable all its net features, separate from Atlantis and Termana or not, and double check all the safety protocols are in place.

Then, I let the message open.

A Drennar woman with the side of her head shaved smiles at me from the screen. Bright blue striations move in her green eyes, and black wings flutter behind her.

But the smile disarms me more than feathers or shifting irises ever could.

Drennar don't smile… Not in any of the videos we have of them.

Warily, I let the video play, fully aware that I may have to throw the whole device out if there turns out to be some hidden bug in this message.

"Hello, Olivia," the Drennar says, but not in her own tongue. She speaks the common human language, perfect and without accent.

It startles me, and I pause the video abruptly.

Beside me, Ricardo stirs. He tightens his grip on me and turns his face toward the laptop. "Gah… So bright."

"Sorry," I whisper, adjusting the brightness of my screen. "I didn't mean to wake you."

"'S alright," he mumbles. "Why are you up so early?"

I stare down at him, watching as he blinks the sleep from his eyes. His gaze alights on the screen, on the pale grey Drennar face staring at us with a genuine smile. He sits up, pulling his arm from my lap and leaning closer to the screen.

"What the fuck?"

"I don't know," I say. "She sent me a message." He sits up, reclining against the wall beside me, and I hasten to add, "This device is secure, don't worry. I'm not watching this on the net just in case they bugged it."

He nods slowly, pursing his lips. "I'm glad you thought about that, because I didn't." He pulls in a deep breath and tips his head to the side. "Why is she… smiling?"

I shrug and shake my head. Then, I resume the video.

"I'm Rone Vargen. You obviously don't know me, but I feel like I know you. I've seen so much footage of you over the years which… feels wrong now. And your father has told me so much about you. That part doesn't feel wrong though."

I pause the video again, brows furrowing.

My father? She knows my dad?

My heart stutters in my chest, and my lungs falter. Tears blur the screen.

Is he… alive?

My hands rise to cover my mouth.

Ricardo sits stone-still beside me. "What is this?" he asks.

But I have no answer for him.

From the screen, the winged Drennar smiles, frozen in place. Her short hair has paused mid-flutter, tickling her chin as she shook her head, assuring me that hearing about me from Dad didn't feel wrong.

He talks about me?

But I'm not what he remembers. I've fallen so far.

Finally moving, Ricardo wraps an arm around me. "It's okay," he says. "Let's see what she has to say."

A thought lets the woman continue her small nod, and she goes on. "For part of one of the experiments," Rone says, wrinkling her nose, "your father and I were shown footage of the attack on Odyssey. And it hurt. I couldn't bear to see Reginald like that."

Genuine pain tightens Rone's eyes, so out of place on a Drennar. The casual use of his name rather than some arbitrarily assigned number, or even his last name, shocks me.

"Anyway, I told him I could get you a message. I never thought to before because... Well, that's a very long story, and Reginald is chomping at the bit to speak with you."

A deep laugh sounds beside her.

"What?" she asks, smiling again. Her eyes sparkle as she looks at the man who laughed, the man I can't let myself believe is my father.

"Chomping at the bit?" he repeats, and the voice rings clear in all my memories.

But it can't be.

"That's a phrase Humans use, isn't it?" Rone asks.

"It used to be. We don't have horses anymore."

"Horses? What do horses have to do with it?" Rone shakes her head, sending her short black hair flying. "Never mind. We can discuss that later. I won't keep you waiting any longer."

She reaches toward me, and I lean back, half expecting their advanced technology to let her reach right through the screen. But she doesn't. Her hand moves below whatever records her, and then the view changes.

Oh my god...

Though a good deal older, I'd know that face anywhere. Crow's feet crinkle the tawny skin around his eyes. Blue permeates brown depths, a warm, inviting hazel, just like mine. Gray streaks through his short brown hair.

"Dad?" I whisper, though I know he can't hear me.

A sad smile spreads his lips, and a sigh lifts his shoulders. "Olivia..."

Shockwaves spread through me, bringing ancient memories careening into focus.

How long have I wanted to hear his voice?

Tears spill over, cascading down my cheeks.

"I wanted so badly to send this message, but now... Where do I even start?" he begins. "I sat down to do this a few times, but what can I even say?"

Dad shakes his head. His mouth opens, but no words come out. He looks up at the ceiling in his bright room. A hand, maybe Rone's hand, touches his back, moving in slow circles. He looks to his side, looks to *her*, and nods.

Rubbing a hand over his face, he clears his throat. "Olivia... I hope you're okay. I'm so sorry, baby girl."

The corners of my eyes prick with new tears, and my lip quivers.

"I never meant for things to go the way they did. I thought... I thought going in your place would be better. I thought you'd have a life, and your mom would move on. I'm so sorry."

Tears trickle over his cheeks, and he wipes them away quickly.

"I thought I was doing what was best. I just didn't know... I didn't know your mom would..."

A sob erupts from me.

On the screen, my father pinches the bridge of his nose. "I didn't know," he says. "But what else could I do? I couldn't let them take you. He had you, and I just... I couldn't."

My throat tightens.

He stares down below the camera for a moment, shaking his head slowly. When he finally looks up, agony carves deep lines in his forehead. "Please, just let me know you're okay, somehow. With everything your mother did, with everything you've gone through... Please, tell me you're alright."

Fresh tears pour over his dark skin, and he takes a moment to compose himself. Ricardo cradles me against him, holding me tight as I sob.

He's been watching me? He's seen footage of me?

He's alive?

My heart clenches, waiting for him to speak.

At long last, he clears his throat. "I'm so proud of the woman you've become, Olivia. I'm proud of you for standing up to your mom. The things she did…" He wipes the tears away, shaking his head. "I'm proud of you. Please, please, let me know you're okay. We can trust Rone. Let her know. Something. Anything."

My throat tightens, and my heart twists.

"I love you, Olivia."

A sob bursts out of me, and though I know he can't hear me, I choke out, "I love you too, Dad."

The tear-blurred image on the screen shifts as Rone moves closer to my father, wrapping her arms around him. He leans into her, pressing his forehead against hers, and the footage stops.

Ricardo tightens his embrace, and I fall to pieces.

***

I tip my head back against my chair and close my eyes. At my request, my Link tells me the time. 8:58 a.m. My meeting hangs over me, meant to set up training times so Atlantis doesn't rest on my shoulders alone.

But my father's message plays over and over in my head.

A million times, I recall the tears on his cheeks. The crinkled lines around his eyes sprawl across my mind like tree roots, twining in and out of every fiber of me.

He's alive.

He's alive, and he tried to talk to me.

I sniff, desperately trying not to cry. The timestamp of his message stings me. It was waiting for me when I tried to kill myself.

Would I have tried if I knew?

The answer is obvious. Of course not.

But, yet again, I wasn't living up to my potential. I wasn't checking on Atlantis. I wasn't maintaining the security system I worked on for fucking years.

I was too busy drinking. Too busy trying to forget. Too busy trying to die.

Too busy failing.

And now, I worry that the potential of wondering how disappointed he'd be if he knew, the pressure of sending a message back, might've pushed me over the edge.

A sigh lifts my shoulders as my Link tells me another minute has passed. I open my laptop, refusing to venture to the

Comm Room in the security offices, refusing to venture out into a world where people stare at me with pity in their eyes.

I glance at the bed, wishing Ricardo still slept there. Or even just that he was still there at all. But he needed food, and I needed privacy for this meeting.

But I need him too. I need him because I don't know what to do.

9:00 a.m.

I command my laptop to connect to the Coalition. They appear on the screen, staring at the wall I know my image hangs on. Introductions and pleasantries drag on, making me ache to be done with this.

My nerves tie themselves into knots, fidgeting with the possible ramifications of this morning. I crack my knuckles, desperate for something to do.

Slowly, I explain the inner workings of Atlantis, stopping to explain even the most basic things to a group of people who've never cared to understand how the tech around them works. They never needed to know, before. Now, with no immediate replacement lined up for my mother or Mulvaney…

It couldn't hurt for them to know.

"Well," Croon says, rubbing his temples, "We can assemble a group of people over the coming days. Shall we plan for their training to begin the day after the…" His hands stop moving, and his gaze rises from the table, fixating on me.

His mouth falls open, moving silently.

Eventually, he says, "I suppose we should give you a few days after the executions."

But I squirm under the pity in his gaze. I can't take the thought of cutting myself even more slack when that's all I've been doing for years.

"No," I say, cutting off whatever he was about to say. "The day after. I'll train them the day after."

I swallow, trying to appear brave and strong.

Ulric leans closer to Croon and whispers, "Then we could get her out of this mess that much sooner. We have much more… *stable* people available."

I try not to flinch. I try not to show just how much his comment stings.

I try not to let them know just how right he is, but my gaze falls. I shrink into myself.

My eyes drift out of focus, staring through my hands and the keyboard I paid so dearly to have. The hands that held far too many bottles. The keyboard I should have used so much more than I did.

"Olivia?" Croon says, and his tone indicates that he may have tried to garner my attention once or twice already.

Ulric shakes his head.

"Sorry," I say, unable to meet his gaze, even through the screen. "It's been a hell of a morning."

But the words sound like an excuse.

"That's alright," McDonough says, cinnamon eyes shining with compassion. "Was there anything more we should know, any additional qualifications we should look for?"

Sighing, I struggle to pull myself together.

"What we discussed will be fine." I swallow back a lump in my throat, then add, "But there is one other thing I need to talk to you about."

My heart jumps into my throat, hammering my vocal cords into submission in a wild attempt to stop me from talking. Because if I don't say it, if I don't tell them, maybe it isn't real.

But the Coalition waits. Croon, McDonough, and Chong sit patiently. Ulric taps his meaty fingers on the table.

"I did a sweep of Atlantis this morning, just checking to see what sort of attempts the Drennar made to get in, and... I found something." Deep breath. "My dad... He sent me a message."

Ulric's tapping stops. McDonough's soft brows reach for each other.

And why shouldn't they?

No one has ever been contacted by an abductee before.

"I accessed it securely with some comms equipment from a decommissioned ship. Atlantis is still intact."

A tear pricks at the corner of my eyes as I recall the look on my father's face as he begged me to let him know I was alive.

"He wants me to send him a message. The Drennar know about the attack on Odyssey. They showed him the footage. I don't…" I wipe a hand over my face.

"I don't know why they showed him that, but he wants to know that I'm okay. And the Drennar that helped him send the message, Rone, she was… different. She laughed. She cried. She… felt things. And they acted like they weren't supposed to send the message."

Lifting my gaze to meet theirs, I say, "I don't know if I should send a message back though. I don't know if I can trust what I saw, what the Drennar said." My gut twists. "What if it's a trick?"

The thought of them using my father's image to trick me into contacting them makes me sick. Could they program a computer so convincingly? Could they make a video with feeling?

Because if that's the case, he may not actually be alive.

My soul threatens to shatter within me, fragile and waiting for a single blow.

"Can you contact them securely?" Chong asks, green eyes sparkling intelligently.

"As long as I use the comms equipment that I accessed the message on, yes. It doesn't need to connect to Odyssey or Termana to send a message."

They exchange glances, clearly out of their depth.

Croon turns to me. "I hate to ask this, I'm sure it was very personal, but can we see the message? I only ask because... We may be more impartial. His absence didn't affect us the way it affected you. If it's a trick, we might see it."

I nod, reaching for the comms device. A few settings changes, and it projects the video onto the wall beside me. I turn my laptop, allowing them the sight of Rone and my father.

Every crack in his voice, every tear in his eyes slams into me. I scrunch my face up, desperate not to break in front of them as I await their decision, wait for them to answer the question burning inside me.

Is this a cruel trick? Or is my dad really alive?

Chapter Thirty Two
Novay

Rone

Lustran wakes quickly, eyes snapping open. He gazes up at the pale ceiling for a long while, but his chest rises and falls faster than it should at a rest. His brows furrow, and his hands clench. Hanging through openings in the alonarium table he rests upon, his wings flutter restlessly.

"Was the surgery successful?" he asks, voice rising just a touch with a hint of panic. He turns his head toward me, moving too fast, seeking reassurance.

All good signs.

I nod. "It was successful."

"Why is my respiratory system aggravated? What is wrong with my facial muscles? Or rather, all my muscles. They are all tense. Was a nerve damaged in the surgery?"

His voice rises and falls, ebbing with anxiety and flowing with desperation.

I smile.

"There was no damage. Your surgery was successful," I repeat, trying to calm him. I reach out, placing my hands on the arms closest to me. His hands unfurl as he teases the tension out of them.

I explain, "Human expressions regarding emotion are… strangely accurate. The body responds instinctively to emotion. It wasn't just idle words."

Lustran holds my gaze, eyes wide with horror. "How many of their expressions have you tested? Are they all accurate? Can these emotions actually cause us pain?"

I smile at his use of the Human language for its expressive nature, and at his use of an excessive word. *Actually*. Something so small, but so tightly linked to emotion in ways we never guessed.

His ears blink rapidly, picking through the findings that I've uploaded.

But I nod, saving him time. "I haven't tested *all* their expressions," I say, leaving out the fact that I haven't been actively testing them at all, that I've just been experiencing them with Reginald. "But they seem to be real. And yes, emotions can be physically painful."

My lips drip into a frown, recalling all the pangs of loss and grief, the desperate clenching of my jaw, the twisted knots in my stomach making me feel ill. My brows furrow as I remember each experience that caused those sensations.

Falling to my knees with Reginald, weeping and sobbing until my throat ached, as we waited to learn if Olivia survived the attack on Odyssey.

Trying to maintain objectivity in the face of the suffering in the experiment on Gordeky, fighting the urge to tell them to go to Meruna, to find the prism they call a gem, the tool that can reprogram the dictator.

Lustran watches my face morph as all these things burst through my mind, but he can't possibly guess the causes. His own face contorts, twisted by fear.

"How can they have such power over the rest of the body?" he asks. "They're such simple functions."

He said they're instead of they are.

His first contraction.

It's almost cute.

"I don't know," I say. "It seems we'll have to find out."

***

I stare up at Lustran, nearly a full meter taller than me, watching as his face contorts. He stares out at the sea of Drennar gathered in the Facility Center with dawning horror. It's the first time he's been here since his operation.

Did I react the same way?

I recall the footage and watch myself walk to my pedestal, hands fidgeting before me. I see the Drennar around me take notice, scanning my twiddling thumbs with academic interest.

And I see myself shrink from them.

Horror didn't shift across my features. Fear did.

Saving the footage for later, I return my attention to Lustran. Silently, I vow to make his acclimatization to emotion easier. His brows scrunch together, watching them all.

"Is this… Is this really what we're like, what we do?"

I tip my head to the side, wondering at him. "What do you mean?"

Surely, he already knew that. He's been doing this, coming to the Facility Center all day, every day, since his release from his maturation tube with only a few exceptions.

Namely, his trip to Termana twelve years ago.

"I just…" His shoulders lift, then fall with a deep sigh. "I thought for some reason that I'd have some sort of… adventure. That seeing all these worlds that we've accessed, learning all about them would be… exciting. But we just stand here, vacant and hollow."

I glance back at the mass of Drennar before us, letting my eyes drift to the empty spots waiting for us within the grid.

294

Our pedestals have yet to come forth, and now, I don't want them to.

I hadn't thought of it quite how Lustran did, hadn't been taken aback by the dullness of our existence. Perhaps the experiments he oversees haven't quite forced him to confront the true horror of us just yet.

I scan his files, and suddenly, that aspect makes sense. His primary experiment is that of Elizabeth Croon and the young people she shares a living space with. They haven't suffered as Reginald has, haven't been tormented.

They spend their days together, growing and developing friendships and romances. They ask constantly about other worlds, and apparently their interest has spread to Lustran.

Another quick sweep reveals that Lustran has been watching old Human movies and shows about space travel or worlds with magic.

"What are we?" he whispers.

And I have no answer for him.

Joo kai isvane coom Isvens.
–We are strong with Allies.–

Chapter Thirty Three
Venice Space Research Station

Krona

Huddled in what the Humans might call a spacious meeting room, Tenna and I sit with our families, letting our highest-ranking warriors spend time with the remnants of their families today. Tension fills us as we rush to prepare for a war we never anticipated. The information Olivia sent us so far tells us only how outmatched we are, and doubt plagues me.

Are we equal to this task?

Will we fall at the hands of our ancestors?

With yet another day of attempted strategy behind us, yet another day lost, my spirits fall. I glance at the people around us, the people gathered to advise us, and see frowns and furrowed brows.

The Coalition's final question from yesterday echoes through my mind. "Do you have any allies we could call upon?"

Our answer was uncertain.

Taron Tribe always did well by us in the past. They never cheated us. They warned us of incoming attacks from Vaerkin with smoke signals.

But would they trust us now? Would they lend us aid?

If we go home with this Sootvali, this star-sickness, this technology, in our arms and in our heads… If we descend from Skon ris Soons, the Realm of Stars, will they still be our allies?

Or will they shun us for fear of catching star-sickness themselves?

Vaerkin might keep a wary distance, avoiding us for the same fear of contamination. Or so I hope. For if Taron Tribe forsakes us, we'll lose access to their weapon-making skills.

My mind swirls uneasily, struggling to come up with something, anything, to boost the spirits of those around me. Never before has it been so hard. Never before have the circumstances been so dire or the stakes quite so high.

Tenna squeezes my hand under the table, lending me her strength. I look to her, staring into moss-green eyes. One corner of her mouth lifts, and she says, "We'll find a way, just like we always do. Daen Tribe is strong."

I nod and squeeze her hand.

I cast my mind over all that's happened since we were stolen away from Regonia and know that she's right. We've overcome more in the past few weeks than I ever could've thought possible to endure.

And I know, we're strongest with our allies.

"We must reach out to Taron Tribe," I say. "We may be sootfenlar," *star-touched*, "but they are not rash. They may allow us to plead our case. And they deserve to know, just in case the Drennar come for them."

Tenna considers my words, nodding slowly.

***

Morning comes too quickly, rapping on my eardrums with the desperate beeping of an alarm. Tenna and I dress for another day on Termana, then meet Olivia and Ricardo in the hangar bay.

My heart aches as soon as I see the hollowness in Olivia's eyes, because I know her fight. The war inside nearly tore me apart years ago, and now, it ravages her mind, her heart.

Reaching out, I pull her toward me. Tenna joins the effort, reaching for her as well. Tugging Ricardo along, we embrace.

"Joo kai isvane coom Isvens," I whisper. We are strong with Allies.

***

A smile crinkles Johnathan Croon's eyes when I tell him we'll contact Taron Tribe once we get to Regonia.

"Do you think they'll help?" he asks. Relief and hope ooze from him.

"We don't know," Tenna says. "For so many winters, we've gazed at the stars with horror. Our ancestors supposedly died of Sootvali, star-sickness. But you say it's just this?" She gestures at her Link. "It's just technology, modifications. And now, *we* wear it. They might attack us on sight. They might barricade their settlement, blocking us out. Or they might see that the danger lurking in the Realm of Stars was always the Drennar."

"They haven't seen what we've seen," I add. "Our experience here has shown us, firsthand, that things aren't what we once thought they were."

Chapter Thirty Four
Termana

Olivia

"We could show them," I say, finally lifting my gaze from the table. I look to Krona and Tenna beside him. For what feels like the first time in weeks, my mind moves quickly, brushing problems aside. "I can take equipment with us. I can download video footage of the Drennar to it."

There's so much I would need to do on Regonia, though.

But the prospect excites me, gives my mind something to do.

"I could show them where the Drennar hid their monitoring devices. I can even disable them if they'd like. I assume you'll want that done with all the tech they left in your village?"

Tenna and Krona answer in unison, "Yes."

My heart glows, warming to the idea of getting my hands on genuine Drennar tech, on the idea of exploring the stars, Skon ris Soons, as the Regonians call it.

Suddenly, life looks a little less bleak.

But Ulric cuts in, "You just assume you're going to Regonia?"

I come up short. "I thought I was…" My voice comes out small.

"Why would *you* go?" Ulric snaps. Anger creases his jowls as he turns in his chair to stare at the other Coalition members. "Of all people, I'm supposed to trust a fucking alcoholic to do this?"

Ricardo takes my hand and says, "*Recovering* alcoholic."

The distinction, that phrase falling from Ricardo's lips stings me, even as his defense, paltry as it may be, buoys my resolve.

I'm a recovering alcoholic.

Fuck, I'm an alcoholic.

I'd known it, deep down. I knew the trap I was walking into every time I took a drink.

But putting a name to it makes it real.

"Oh, that's so much better," Ulric says, pursing his lips. He turns to me with acid in his eyes. "How long's it been since your last drink? A day?"

I drop my gaze, faltering before him. My voice sneaks out of me on a whisper, "Five days."

But I know it isn't long enough.

"Five days?! Really? That's supposed to make me trust you enough to fly out of the solar system?"

Croon leans toward Ulric, silver hair sweeping forward over his face. "Terrence, this is not the time, nor the way, to handle this."

But Ulric continues, undaunted. "That's supposed to make me trust you to deliver our allies to Regonia to recruit more people for our war? I'm supposed to trust you with the future of my wife and kids? Why the fuck should I trust *you* with this?"

Tears prick at the corners of my eyes, blurring the room around me. "Because you don't have a choice," I whisper. "Every other pilot that could fly SCFS class ships were recruited by my mother and Mulvaney."

"Well, then, we'll just have to get someone else certified," he sputters. "Sending you is asking for disaster."

"Ulric!" Croon demands. "This is NOT appropriate."

"Neither is sending a suicidal alcoholic as an emissary to a race that values strength!" Ulric shouts. His reflection in the shiny metal table turns red. "They won't ally themselves with us if *she* is what they know of us."

My tears drip onto the table, but I keep myself still, hoping no one will notice.

But beside me, Krona and Tenna rise to their feet. Tenna moves to stand behind me, and Krona puts his hands on the table, leaning forward over it. The thick metal groans beneath his weight.

Silence descends on the room, and my sniffling screams against it. Ricardo pulls me to him, and Tenna rests gentle hands on my shoulders.

"Olivia is not weak," Krona growls. "The war inside is brutal and merciless. It obeys no code of conduct, no restrictions. The war she fights is fierce. She is a warrior in her own right."

Tears fall in earnest, and my shoulders shake viciously. Tenna moves her hand in comforting circles on my back.

But Ulric doesn't back down, not completely. Continuing at a more normal volume, he says, "She tried to kill herself. The only reason she failed is because *he* found her and dragged her sorry ass to the hospital."

Tenna's hands desert me, and a sudden screech of the table screams for my attention. Leaning across the table, Krona stares hard into Ulric's eyes. The Minister of Treasury and Commerce sweats beneath his gaze.

"Krona," Tenna whispers, tugging at his arm.

Slowly, he rises to his full height, leaving Ulric to swallow back a lump of fear.

306

"Ricardo played his role in saving Olivia's life, this is true," Tenna says. "But she had the foresight to plan for the tougher battles, using your tech to her advantage. She programmed her Link to send a distress call. Battles are not often won by chance. Forethought and backup plans are necessary, a thing that *she* understands. Our people will not think her weak for this. We have known the war inside. We have felt grief and loss."

Ricardo kisses the top of my head, soft and gentle. The gesture combines with Tenna's words to pull still more tears from my eyes, blurring the sight of Ulric's shocked expression.

"If you cannot see the importance of forethought and contingency plans," Tenna says, "then you have no place in this room or in any discussions involving war."

Rising to my feet, I throw my arms around Tenna and Krona, weeping openly. "Thank you," I croak.

***

The four of us sit quietly in Sparrow, slipping through daet Skon ris Soons.

The Realm of Stars.

The name floats through my head, smooth and silky. I urge Sparrow to play a song for us, and "Staying Power by Emma Ruth Rundle. 2020" comes on. The reverberating rumble at the beginning of the song shakes the cabin, and Ricardo turns to me.

"Is there something wrong with the ship?" he asks.

The guitar kicks in, sparing me the need for explanation.

"Oh," he says with a chuckle. "Never mind."

I glance at him, and I want to smile. I want to return the sweet expression of joy that glows upon his face.

But the pain I've caused everyone, the fact that I'm their last choice for a pilot, the fact that I didn't even realize it until this morning… It all fills my head, drowning me, and I just want to stop thinking for a minute.

Did I really have to dump all my alcohol out?

Couldn't I have saved back a bit, just for a tough day?

I shake my head.

Stop it! It wouldn't just be one drink. It wouldn't just be one day.

I glance at Ricardo as we approach Venice Station, and his smile runs away. His eyes soften sympathetically. The airlock opens for us, and I set Sparrow down in the hangar. The turntable rotates beneath us, granting me a fleeting glimpse of the Realm of Stars as the door closes.

Tenna, Krona, and Ricardo unfasten their belts, preparing to disembark. Their stomachs grumble, eagerly anticipating the dinner that awaits us. But I stare out the window at the airlock door.

A gentle hand comes to rest on my shoulder, but I don't look up. "Are you okay?" Ricardo asks, voice soft.

"I just…" I trail off, looking for words. "I just need a minute."

"Do you want me to stay with you or do you want to be alone?"

"Yeah."

Ricardo chuckles. "It's more of an either/or type of question," he teases.

Dropping my gaze to the controls before me, I nod, acknowledging my mistake. The latest of many. "Stay? I mean… if you want. You don't have to."

He settles back into his seat, what would be the co-pilot's seat if I needed one for this class of ship, reaching out a hand. Our fingers lace together, resting on my leg.

Over his shoulder, he tells Tenna and Krona that we'll be along soon. Then, the music falls over us, unbroken by our words. I stare at the controls, contemplating opening the hangar door as soon as Krona and Tenna are safely beyond the airlock.

"Do you think we can do this?" Ricardo asks. "The war with the Drennar, I mean."

I consider everything, piecing the facts together in my head. Our history plays out, a highlight reel of devastation. The violence and wreckage of wars past and wars to come smolder in my thoughts.

"I don't have much faith in humanity, but our ability to destroy things is undeniable," I whisper. I meet his gaze and nod. "We can break the Drennar. We just don't know how yet." Turning to face the hangar door, I add, "Or how many lives it'll cost us."

I let my head fall back against the headrest and stare forward at the solid metal holding me back from the Realm of Stars. A quick scan of nearby Link access points finds Krona and Tenna speaking with their families, still in the hangar.

So, I leave the door in place.

My mind fills with today's events. Ulric's disapproval screams in my head, but Krona's and Tenna's defenses sing louder.

"I think I might see if I can live here, with Daen Tribe," I say. "You can still stay in my room on Odyssey, if you want." Then, nervously, I add, "Or... you could come to Venice, too. It'll be cramped quarters. We'd probably have to bunk together. But I just..."

A lump forms in my throat, and I struggle to swallow it back. "I want to be with Tenna and Krona. I want to be with Daen Tribe, learning about them and Regonia."

My mind aches for something new, something to learn, to challenge me. Boredom edges every day, leaving room for my mind to strangle me, but the thought of an entire planet to learn about sparks a fire within me.

Something to stay alive for, maybe.

Ricardo stares at me in my periphery, but I can't meet his gaze. I can't bear whatever expression might haunt his eyes, be it rejection or pity.

Because I know my attempt to shield my true intentions is thin.

He must know I want him here with me.

"I think I'd rather be on Venice," Ricardo says. His voice comes out husky, but he clears his throat.

I turn to look at him, desperate to glean some sort of meaning from his expression now that I know the answer is favorable.

His tone lightens, and he adds, "Staying in your room without you just seems... creepy."

Despite myself, I smile. "It'd only be creepy if you dug through my drawers looking for my underwear or something."

311

"You wear underwear? I had you pegged for a commando type. Maybe I will stay on Odyssey to look for them."

I laugh and roll my eyes, gently nudging him with my elbow. A blush creeps over my skin, warming me.

Because for all his joking, he's already seen my underwear once.

The night we met flashes through my mind, a haze of skin and questing lips, alcohol and terrible news, gentle touches and hungry kisses.

Will I ever know what it's like with him… sober?

Ricardo smiles brazenly, one eyebrow quirked up, and I wonder if he's thought about that night since then. There have been so many opportunities, but I can't exactly blame him for passing.

I'm already dead weight, clinging to him for dear life. Why would he want to make that burden heavier, more complicated?

My mind whirls, scolding me for such mean-spirited thoughts. He deserves to be thought of better.

He's just too good, too nice, to take advantage of the shipwreck I've become.

Chapter Thirty Five
Novay

Rone

So little time has passed since the others received their modifications, mere days, yet we have our own budding community. Our petition to live as the group Elizabeth Croon lives with passed quickly, and now, I lie awake in my bed, smiling at the sounds of bodies moving beyond my open door.

Several Drennar converse in the living area that serves as a hub for all our private quarters, and I listen. I pay no mind to the words they speak, only the undertones, the laughter that punctuates their conversations. Pauses, heavy with meaning, spark my interest. Hushed tones prick at my ears, begging me to tune into the audio devices in that room.

But I resist, satisfied to hear the emotion in their voices.

Pulling in a deep breath, I smile. I tug my blanket up over me, inhaling deeply because it isn't actually my blanket. The scent of Reginald fills my nose, and I'm suddenly thankful that I switched them.

I can't bring him here, but I can have a reminder of him.

My smile brightens as I realize what I've done, the sentimentality of this action. I push away the implications, happy to lay here for the time being, relaxed and serene.

But I only have a few moments to enjoy it.

I'll be expected at my pedestal within half an hour. I need to turn my data stream back to unlimited and sync up to prepare myself.

Before these modifications, I would've climbed from bed immediately, mind awash with the data of the morning, with the evening's data already assimilated. I'd have gone about my morning routine mechanically, reaching my pedestal at the exact same moment as every day that came before.

But not today.

Today, I content myself with a quick view of Reginald. The camera in his room finds him still asleep, reminding me just how much longer Humans need to rest.

A dreamy smile plays over his lips, and I pull in a deep breath. Nestling into the blanket that smells of him, I let myself drift off to sleep again.

After all, I don't have to be at my pedestal for another twenty-seven minutes.

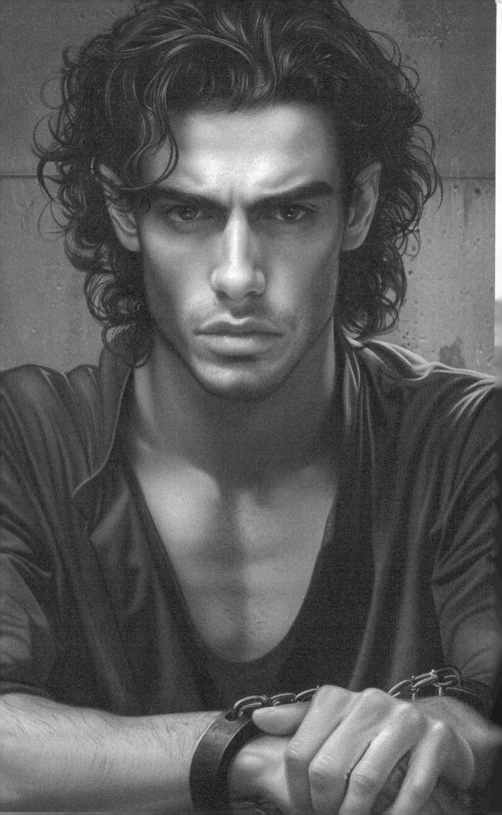

Chapter Thirty Six
Odyssey Space Research Station

Ricardo

I send a quick message to Francis, sending the first thing that comes to mind, desperate to distract myself from the meeting I know is coming.

Olivia's away, meeting with Cait, and I sit alone on her bed. I turn music on as I wait for Francis to reply, falling back on the comfortable mattress as "The Call of the Iron Peak by The Devil's Trade. 2020" breathes out through the speakers.

My Link flashes a warm amber, and I have my cochlear implant read it for me.

"All the prisoner transfers happened already. They came and got these bastards the day after the attack on Odyssey. I thought you knew that…"

Of course, I know that. But nothing better came to mind. So, I send back, "Just making sure. I didn't want to leave Termana with any of them still hiding out."

It's a lame excuse.

Another message comes in. "You know, you can just say you're nervous, right?"

I chuckle.

Damn it, Francis.

I send back, "I know." But I freeze, unable to come up with anything more after that.

But I don't have to. Within a few heartbeats, another message lights up my Link as Francis apparently senses my need to talk.

"Are you excited to go to Regonia?"

I kick myself mentally for not thinking of such an obvious topic. "I really am. The thought of setting foot on a real planet, of seeing another world, a *real* world... It's amazing."

"Well," her next message reads, "I'd be terrified. I'm glad it's you, not me. Especially since Giselle and I *just* found a partner couple."

"Oh, I forgot to tell you! I met Nico. He seems really nice. I haven't met his partner, though." Then, in a rush, I add, "I'm glad it's me going, too. Especially since it means I'll get some more time with Olivia."

I glance at the room, at the tapestries and little trinkets on the shelves, and a smile brightens my features. My eyes linger on all the little things that survived so long, the things sturdy enough to have held up since Humans left Earth.

Another message from Francis comes through, cutting off my gentle musings.

"You've been spending a lot of time with her since she..."

My heart grinds to a stop at the mention of Olivia's attempted suicide.

My Link glows, and I stare at the next message.

"I just... I know you're good for her. But is she good for you? I don't want to sound cold, I know the heart wants what it wants, but... She's already put you through so much. And she clearly has a drinking problem. You already dealt with that so much with your parents."

Another message.

"I guess I'm just worried about you. Just take care of yourself. If you say she's good for you, if you say this is good

318

for you, then I'll support you. But you need to at least think about whether this is going to hurt you more in the long run."

My chest tightens, and my stomach drops. I gulp down a breath, trying to steady myself, all to no avail.

But Olivia isn't like my mother.

All our late-night conversations come rushing back to me, reminding me just how much effort she put into doing things right, even when she wanted to dive into the bottle more and more.

"Olivia isn't my parents." I send the message, then quickly realize that I need to explain. So, I send another.

"She isn't standing by, lost in an alcoholic haze as her children are abused. Even when she was drinking the most, she still set alarms and made sure to be sober for meetings and flights. She didn't drink while making her new defense program. She only drank when she thought no one would be hurt by it. She only tried to—"

A tear trickles over my cheek as I remember finding her in Sparrow, limp and lolling in her chair with the bottles at her feet. I cut the message off, unable to see it on my Link screen. I send it and start another message.

"She only did that when she thought she wasn't needed anymore. She stuck around until then. She just didn't know we still need her, that we still want her. And anyway, she's getting help, now. My parents never would've done that."

A long moment passes before Francis' reply comes through. "They definitely wouldn't have. I hope I didn't upset you too much. I just know how you are. You don't think about yourself."

I can almost see the softening of her eyes, glowing beneath red hair. It certainly isn't the only thing that makes Francis so unique. Her perception is unrivalled.

But I have somewhere terrible to be.

So, I say, "I know. My best and worst quality. I have to go though. Thanks for distracting me."

A curt, "Anytime," comes through, and I roll off the bed. Shutting the music off as the door slides open, I step out into the hall to meet Olivia at the hangar.

***

My palms sweat as I wait outside a security room on Washington Station. Olivia sits beside me, fidgeting with the hem of her shirt. I reach out, placing a gentle hand on her arm.

But before I can say a word, a Soldier steps into the room, Link flashing as she receives several messages. She never breaks eye contact, never so much as raises an eyebrow at whatever they contain.

"Specialist Bourdeau," she says.

Still adjusting to my new title, having never expected to jump a couple ranks in so short a time, I blink slowly. Someone who would have outranked me just days ago now stands at attention in my presence. Looking up at her from my chair, I nod.

"We're ready for you, sir."

Rising from my chair, I turn to Olivia. "I, uh… I guess I'll be, well, not *right* back. I'll be back soon."

"Okay," she answers, voice small.

As I follow the Soldier to an interrogation room, I hear another voice tell Olivia that they're ready for her, but I don't hear her response. My heart hammers my eardrums more and more fiercely with every step. The short hall seems to stretch for an eternity, and my gut churns anxiously.

I have to do this…

320

I'll regret it otherwise.

But that doesn't ease the greasy feeling in the pit of my stomach. It doesn't lessen the strain, doesn't soothe my nerves.

When the Soldier opens the door to the interrogation room, holding it open to allow me passage, my breath leaves me.

In the middle of an otherwise empty room, my brother sits. Handcuffs lock him in place, chaining him to a sturdy metal loop welded to the metal table before him.

My heart breaks, shattering into a million pieces. Tears prick at the corners of my eyes as I stare at him, just as skinny as he's always been. He stares at the table before him, and condescension burns in his eyes.

"Oh great..." he drawls. "It's you. Goody-two-shoes." His lips purse. "Couldn't have been Angelina..."

Has she not come to say goodbye?

Somehow, that makes me like my sister-in-law just a bit more.

Stepping forward, I let the Soldier close the door behind me. I stare down at my brother, struggling to see the sweet little boy I took so many punches to protect, the carefree kid I made lunches for and walked to school.

But he isn't here anymore.

Some cruel man resides within his body, instead.

"What the fuck do you want, Ricardo?" Ferdinand asks. "Is it time for another lecture? I didn't need you to be my dad when we were kids, and I sure as hell don't need it, now. Why the fuck do you think I haven't talked to you in years?"

I shake my head, astounded.

I thought... I thought he appreciated everything I did for him.

"I just have a question for you," I say, voice hollow. "Why?"

Chapter Thirty Seven
Washington Space Research Station

Olivia

"We're ready for you, Miss Dobovich," the Soldier before me says.

I flinch at my last name, at the reminder of my connection to my mother. For the millionth time, I reconsider this whole thing.

I could just go back to Sparrow. I could sit there and wait for Ricardo.

I certainly don't owe her a visit, not after everything she's done.

Looking up at the Soldier, I force myself to meet his gaze. Warmth radiates from soft brown eyes, granting me the courage to say, "Can I... I mean, do I have to go in, now? Can I have a minute?"

Truth be told, I expected to wait longer. Though I suppose my mother doesn't have many appointments to put ahead of me these days.

"Take all the time you need," the Soldier says.

Without another word, I rise from my chair and wander through the lower level of the station. My mind drifts up the stairs, past the armed Soldiers that stand at every stairwell and elevator guarding the residential section, now a prison.

And every soul in residence is destined for death.

How many families will this tear apart?

How many kids will grow up missing a parent, just like I did?

Though, I suppose I may as well have been missing both parents.

When I reach a window, I stop and stare out at the stars. I barely think the command, but my Link starts playing a song for me. "Her in the Distance by Oceans of Slumber. 2018."

I pull in a deep breath, letting my eyes roam over space dust and distant stars. And I think of my mother.

A deep, unsettling chill seeps into me.

Do I owe her a visit?

Just because she's my mom? Just because she gave birth to me? Does that mean I'm obligated to see her, despite all the shit she put me through?

My mind flings a memory at me, dragging me back into it.

My heart hammers as I listen to my mother say, "Olivia, I don't have time for this. Just do what you're supposed to do. I need to get back to the labs."

I delete all my homework assignments, seething, as my mother turns to leave. Her heels clack on the cold metal floor of our living room.

"Of course, you have to go," I spit. "Why wouldn't you?"

She turns on her heel to face me. "What's that supposed to mean?"

"It means you never spare a second for me. I'm surprised you bothered to talk to me about this in person." Hot tears prick at the corners of my eyes, but I hold them back. My hands ball into fists, nails carving little divots in my palms.

Her mouth falls open, and she prepares to berate me, yet again.

But I'm not done.

"Do you wish they took me instead of Dad?" My voice comes out small, a far cry from the fierce rage I want to slap her with.

"Olivia, don't start this again. Quit crying out for attention all the time. You know I love you."

But her eyebrow raises, and a muscle in her jaw twitches.

Desperate to push, to get her to tell me that she's glad I'm here, I say, "That isn't what I asked."

A single tear trickles over my cheek, betraying me.

My mother clenches her jaw, but sadness moves behind her eyes. She drops her gaze, and I flinch.

Silently, she turns her back on me. Tears pour over my cheeks as she walks away, heading back to the labs, yet again.

Now, staring out at the stars, I wipe away the echoes of those tears, drying my face on my sleeve. Ice moves through my veins, and my heart stutters in my chest.

Did she ever care about me?

Or was it always just Dad?

I try so hard to remember a day since the Drennar took him, even just one, when she smiled at me, when she hugged me, when she even bothered to *pretend* to give a shit.

The night they took him, she tried to save me.

Until Dad gave himself up in my place.

From that moment on, she was lost to me, to everyone.

My thoughts fill with one of the first times I saw Cait.

She sits before me in her tidy office, warm and inviting, smiling sympathetically. "Why do you hack your mother's computers?"

"Because I can?" I reply, not even trying to meet her gaze. I keep my eyes glued to the hem of my loose shirt as I pick at it.

"I don't think that's it," Cait says. "That isn't a good enough reason. Not for you, at least."

"Then why do you think I do it?" I ask, hoping to derail her.

"I think you do it to feel some sort of connection to her."

Even now, the words sting. I lean against the cool glass, letting my forehead rest against it. Wiping away more tears, I cross my arms between myself and the window.

Why am I even here?

A thousand memories flash through my mind. Birthdays spent alone at home. Cooking for myself every night. Maintaining the house, cleaning up, washing her clothes because she was too busy at work to even bother with that.

Shopping, arranging everything for my schooling.

Huddling under my blankets when some drunk guy started pounding on the door in the middle of the night, wishing an adult were there to tell him to get lost. I was only fourteen. He certainly wouldn't have left if I'd told him to go.

Anger courses through me at the memory of my wrecked childhood, at the life Dad gave up so much to protect. But she couldn't be bothered to care.

I grit my teeth, blood boiling.

She just left me.

She left me to fend for myself, after he sacrificed everything.

He didn't know if they'd kill him or torture him or what they'd do, and yet he went. But she couldn't bother to talk to me.

Righteous fury tears through me, and I remember why I came here.

This isn't for her.

This is for me.

Pushing away from the window, I shut off my music and stomp back to the security offices. The same man waits, leaning against a wall and examining his Link. The sound of my footsteps jerks his eyes up to me, and he stands upright abruptly. Taking in the change in my demeanor, he nods and leads me back.

We pass several doors, making our way down a short hall. My feet pound the metal floor, desperate to release some of the tension twisting me into knots. The Soldier stops at the last door, opening it and stepping through ahead of me.

And there she is.

My jaw clenches, even as the sight of her cuffed to the table chills me.

Meekly, she whispers, "I didn't think you'd come."

"Neither did I."

The Soldier shuts the door quietly, then moves to a corner behind me.

A long, slow breath puffs out my chest as I take in the deep wrinkles in my mother's face, the streaks of gray that snuck in when I wasn't looking. Utterly helpless, she stares up at me, pitiful and forlorn.

No.

Don't pity her.

She made her fucking choice.

But the furrow of her brows, so different from the heinous arch in my memories, threatens to soften my resolve.

"Thank you for coming. I was hoping you would," she says.

"I'm not here for you," I spit. "I'm here for me."

I recall every terrible memory of her, remember the times she neglected me, the attack on Odyssey, everything she put Daen Tribe through. I hold onto the rage that filled me mere seconds ago, desperate to say what I know I need to say before this defeated version of my mother robs me of my willpower.

Just like she robbed me of everything else.

"I don't know if I'll regret saying this later, but I know I'll regret *not* saying it. You were a terrible mother. And you're a terrible human being."

Her jaw falls slack, mouth hanging open.

"You didn't care what happened to me after they took Dad. You couldn't even pretend. You were my Mom! You were supposed to fucking *be* there!" My fists shake at my sides. "But that would have taken time away from your precious experiments, your *shitty* legacy."

Heat surges through me, even as a tear slides free of my mother's eyes.

"And you know what the worst part is? You became just as bad as them. You abducted 6,000 people! How can you sleep at night?"

"I was going to take them back!" she exclaims, leaning forward. Tears fall in earnest, and her tone falls to a whisper. "I swear, I was."

"Oh, you were going to take them back? Before or after slaughtering 2,000 of them? Before or after slaughtering everyone on Bolivia Station? Before or after manipulating their minds to use them against the Drennar? Before or after basically ordering my death?" I shake my head, incredulous. "Your own daughter!"

A lump in my throat chokes me, giving her time to say, "I told them to try not to."

"Oh, that makes it so much better."

Her lip quivers, a blurred shape shaking in the sheen of my tears. I wipe them away and twist the knife. "Dad's alive, you know."

She stills, pulling in a sharp breath.

And because I can't help myself, because I need to hurt her as much as she's hurt me, I say, "He's alive on Novay, and he hates the monster you've turned into. And so do I."

Her face falls, and she stares at the table. Lips parted, she shakes her head, slowly. I watch my mother brace her elbows on the table and drop her head into her hands.

And I can't look at her anymore. My eyes dart to the ceiling. "I hate that I love the person you used to be," I say.

Tears fall in rivers, splashing on the floor at my feet. "I hate that you're the parent I got stuck with. I hate that you never cared, and I hate that I *always* did."

Sobs wrack my body, battering my poor heart.

"I hate that I tried so hard to reach for you, that I tried *so hard* to get your attention. I hate that it never worked."

A deep, shuddering breath rattles through me, breaking my voice. My hands shake, and something in me shatters.

And everything comes out.

"I hate that I always felt like it was because I wasn't good enough. I hate that you were so bad at being a mom that I hated myself. And I still do!" I say, voice rising. "I still blame myself for all your fuck-ups. I hate that, despite all of it, despite every-fucking-thing, somehow I still love you, somehow I still need your approval, still need you to think I'm good enough to bother with."

I shake my head wiping the tears away. Finally dropping my gaze from the cold, metal ceiling, I find her staring at me with tears cascading over her cheeks.

And words fail me.

"I'm sorry," she croaks. "I love you, Olivia. I'm so sorry. I wish I could make it better. I wish I could fix it."

Pulling in a deep breath, hating the way my lungs hitch and falter, I say, "It's a little late now, isn't it?"

My throat aches as I turn from her. My fingers tremble at my sides, and my breath comes in shallow, shuddering gasps.

The Soldier opens the door for me, offering up a sympathetic half-smile. It only serves to pull more tears forward. They course over my cheeks, running down my neck to soak my shirt.

And my mother's sobs drown out my footsteps as I walk away.

May we find your Sound.

Efsi

Chapter Thirty Eight
Venice Space Research Station

Tenna

Perched on the bench beneath the window, Olivia and Ricardo glance at each other. Olivia swallows nervously, and worry grows within me. When they showed up, tear-stained and sorrowful, I assumed it was about their family members. But that shouldn't make them nervous.

Has something else gone wrong?

Footsteps sound beyond the open door, and Krona quickly appears. He shuts the door behind him, rushing anxiously toward us.

"Is everything alright?" he asks, sitting beside me on the bed.

"Yeah," Ricardo says quickly. "Sorry. We didn't mean to scare you."

I breathe a sigh of relief, thankful that I have nothing to fear from their visit.

Framed by space, Olivia glances at her lap. "Sorry. I should've thought about this. I should've thought about how you'd react."

Ricardo squeezes her hand, and my heart warms.

"It's no trouble," I hasten to say. "Really."

"What is it you wanted to talk about?" Krona asks.

"I just…" Olivia pauses, pulling in a deep breath. "If it's too much trouble, I understand. I know you're all in pretty close quarters already, but… I just don't want to live on Odyssey anymore." Finally, she meets my gaze, then Krona's. "I completely understand if you don't want me to live here, but I'd… I'd really like to."

"Me, too. If you'll have me," Ricardo adds.

And though Olivia's obvious pain twists my heart, I smile. "Of course!" I exclaim, thrilled at the prospect of having my friends close again. The terror and helplessness of not being able to get to her flickers through my mind, quickly followed by a parade of sleepless nights while she recovered.

Not to mention the simple joy of having them near.

"We would have asked," Krona says, "but we just assumed you'd want to be with the rest of the Humans."

With a derisive laugh, Olivia says, "Humans are terrible creatures."

Though I laugh, I mean every word when I say, "Not all of them."

The air thickens around us, heavy with all the words I didn't have to say.

"We have no spare rooms, but we'll make a partition," Krona says. "It didn't feel right having a room to ourselves while everyone else shared, anyway."

"Are you sure?" Olivia asks, giving us one more chance to back out, to push her away.

But I have no intention of doing that.

"Very sure," I say, nodding for emphasis.

Finally, a smile breaks over Olivia's features. "I'll get everything packed today and tomorrow, then. I'll have to store most of it, but there are a few things I want to make sure I have here."

"Bring whatever you want. You can tell us what all that stuff is," Krona says with a smile.

"Most of it's just old tech," she says. "But I'll tell you about it."

My Link flashes with an incoming message, and so does Krona's, drawing our attention away from the conversation.

"It's Croon," Krona says.

He answers his message, wrapping an arm around me and draping his other arm over our laps so that I might see his Link.

Silver hair slicked back, Johnathan Croon stands in the cafeteria on Washington Station. Behind him, lab technicians flip switches on the sides of the doomed beds. Unconscious Humans lie within them with wires connected to various parts of their bodies.

White patches adorn their skin, some rest where Links used to be, others on necks and skulls. I scrunch my brows, trying to figure out what they might have had there.

"We're running a bit behind. We expect to begin at 1:30 rather than noon," he says.

We nod and thank him for letting us know. He rushes off, saying he has a lot to do still and promising to contact us later in the day.

As soon as the video message closes, I look to Olivia and Ricardo. They stare at the floor. My stomach turns at the betrayal they must feel knowing that their own family was party to this, or even a driving force behind it. The hurt Olivia must carry, knowing her mother sanctioned her death, twists my heart.

Krona pulls in a deep breath, and I wonder if he's thinking of the betrayal those particular Humans planted in his mind. I squeeze his hand, hating that he saw that image of me, saw me tarnished in such an act. But those false memories have been removed, the chemical processes reversed.

338

Watching Olivia and Ricardo, my lips droop into a frown. Their families betrayed them, betrayed their entire race, and it's no false memory implanted in an experiment.

It's real.

And it isn't going anywhere.

**

Sitting in the cafeteria with all the surviving members of our Tribe, I luxuriate in the sounds of 4,000 voices, 4,000 sets of feet and hands, 4,000 lives. We move together, humming and singing, stomping and pounding fists against palms.

The demand for justice moves through us.

Our hearts beat as one, and we gasp for breath together. We raise our voices in a shout, letting the fury of unavenged deaths burn through us.

But the time draws near.

Screens all around the room come to life, painting the walls the colors of bodies in beds, hooked up to the same wires they used to kill our family, our friends. Technicians move from bunk to bunk, securing the star-sickness in place.

In our ears, through the magic of the Link and the implants, we hear Johnathan Croon's speech, lamenting such tragic circumstances. All of Termana, the entire Human population, has the option to watch him, to watch us, right now.

Beside me, Krona shouts, voice rising above those of our fellows. I join him, feeling the swell and sway of all our people. I stomp three times, and he follows suit. Surrounding us, our families stomp three times.

And the sound carries outward like a wave, rippling through the crowd as each person stomps, joining in at the exact right moment.

Krona and I raise our voices in an eerie wail, voices careening dangerously high.

And all at once, we stop.

Silence falls around the cafeteria immediately, raising the hairs on my arms in anticipation.

Johnathan Croon says nothing more, and the screens lining the walls course with electricity. The sounds of arms and legs flailing against bed railings and restraints fills the air as the Soundless come to justice.

I'll find your sound, my brother, just as I brought death unto your killer.

I watch them shake as the instrument of their design rattles their bodies. The buzz of electricity fills the gaps between hollow thuds as they twitch.

When the last heartbeat fades, a technician flips a switch, and the bodies fall limp.

Relief flows through me.

***

I sit with my legs crossed beneath me in our quarters. Krona settles in behind me, placing one leg on either side of mine. The warmth of him soaks into me, granting me strength.

My parents settle in across from me, side by side, equal in their grief. Kala sits beside me. Her partner, Melnara, kisses the top of her head as she scoots forward against Kala's back, putting one leg on either side of her.

I glance at my sister, at the woman who fought alongside me in many battles, ferocious and strong. The tears shining upon her dark gray skin pull a lump into my throat. I reach for her hand and give it a squeeze. She nods, and the corners of her lips lift into a sad smile.

On my other side, the space that should have been occupied by Rimahn, Efsi's partner, sits empty. We'll mourn her next, after her family finds her sound.

We'll mourn friends and warriors. We'll mourn family and mentors.

The scope of our loss spreads out before me, a gaping hole where just over 2,000 lives used to be. My heart twists in my chest, flinching at the agony of so many senseless deaths.

My lungs falter at the prospect of all we've learned, all our beliefs laid bare for the cruel trickery they sprang from.

But a fierce determination simmers in my belly.

We will see the Drennar brought to justice for their misdeeds, whatever they may be, as many as they may be, just as we saw the foulest members of the Human race brought to justice today. A small ache builds within me, knowing that Olivia and Ricardo must suffer, even now.

But that is a hurdle for another day.

Today, I find Efsi's sound.

A sob wracks my body.

Krona rubs his hands over my arms and kisses the back of my head. Though I know he wishes to speak, to comfort me, he says nothing. The sounds uttered here shall come only from my parents, my sister, and I.

I look to my parents, letting my eyes trace the tears that stain their cheeks. Their hands lay together, resting atop knees that just touch.

I pull in a deep breath as my mother nods, and I fill my mind with Efsi.

His gentle smile, his clever eyes. The confidence he always held for those around him, pushing everyone to their best.

I hear his laugh, feel its deep timbre shake my bones.

Memories of our childhood flood me, and I see us running in the fields with Kala and playing with the little furry gestans that took shelter in our stables. I concentrate not on my part of the memory, but his.

Instead of my own feelings in those moments, I try to feel his. Rather than my own thoughts, I try to imagine what his might have been.

And I bring him closer to me, seeing the world through his eyes.

The sincere joy of a child playing with gestans, the exuberance of a grown man who maintained that simple joy, the dedication of a warrior and a brother...

These things show me a clearer version of my brother than I've ever seen before.

And I begin searching for his sound.

A gentle susurration eases past my lips, but it doesn't feel like him. Moving into a higher pitch, I try to find that hope that always guided him, and I come close.

Kala joins in beside me, rolling the sound, but it becomes too hard. My parents mimic our sound, changing it, softening it.

The gentle purr of a mother gesta cooing for her babies comes to mind, and I utter it, feeling the way my lungs reverberate with it, the way my heart soars at the sound.

It's him.

Kala and our parents join me, drawing the sound out as our hearts beat together. Tears flow over my cheeks, but my voice never stops.

We've found him.

Chapter Thirty Nine
Odyssey Space Research Station

Olivia

My Link flashes with a message from Johnathan Croon, officially allowing me to send a reply to my father. My heart soars, and butterflies build within me. I've wanted to talk to him for so long.

But what if I'm not what he wants me to be?

I've already disappointed so many people.

My hands tremble at the thought. Or maybe that's the withdrawals.

I grab the salvaged comms unit, one of the few things not yet packed into boxes for my move to Venice. The tiny sphere sits in my cupped palms, waiting for me to command it to life, ready to record my message.

But no words come to mind.

Should I lead with my alcoholism? Or my failed suicide?

Or maybe I should tell him that I turned his wife, my own mother, over to the Coalition, to be executed?

At least I don't have to tell him what she did...

Sighing, I steal a glance at the bathroom door. The water stops, and I keep myself from imagining the drops tracing Ricardo's well-honed physique, however pleasant or distracting that train of thought may be.

I don't have room in my head for that right now. I need to figure out what to say to Dad.

Rising from my chair, I tuck the comms device away on one of the shelves. With one final glance at the bathroom door, I slip out of my room before Ricardo emerges.

The lights of the hall, far brighter than those of my own room, blind me. I keep my pace even as I wander through halls I've barely traversed since I got out of the hospital. My eyes glue themselves to the cold metal beneath my feet, unwilling to bear the stares of those milling about in the halls, unable to tolerate the barren steel walls.

People move out of my way. A few whisper as I pass, and I catch bits and pieces of their comments.

"Is it true?"

"Did her Dad really—"

"They didn't kill him?"

"What about everyone else they took?"

I walk faster, knowing I don't have answers for them. Not yet. The pressure to send him a message builds, and I try to piece together everything I need to ask.

But my mind boggles at the prospect of so many questions.

I shake my head and turn down an empty hall, heading for the center of the station. But footsteps follow me. I glance over my shoulder.

Ricardo stares at me, brows furrowed and lips pulled into a frown. His damp hair hangs around his face, swaying as he walks toward me.

"Are you stalking me?" I ask, trying to be casual. But Lachlan flashes through my mind, and suddenly, I wonder if my friend turned attacker actually did stalk me at some point.

It startles Ricardo, and he stops a meter away. "No," he says, shaking his head. "It sounds bad when you say it like that. I'm just worried about you. We were supposed to watch a movie, but you just left. The last time you snuck out... you..."

I sigh, only just now remembering our plans. "Sorry," I whisper.

Stepping closer, he wraps his hand around mine. "It's alright. You've got a lot on your mind." His thumb caresses the back of my hand. "We can skip it if you want. We've been spending a lot of time together. I get it if you want to be alone."

But that isn't the problem.

I *need* to be alone. So I don't hurt anyone else. So I'll focus on what I need to do.

But I don't *want* to be alone.

I shake my head and force myself to speak. "Will you come with me?"

A smile lifts the corners of Ricardo's lips, and he nods.

I lead him to the center of the station, letting the warmth of his hand seep into mine. We skirt past the gym and the school room, and I scan my Link at the elevator. It opens for us, and we descend.

When the door opens to the hangar, the lowest level of the station, Ricardo pauses. After a brief hesitation, he follows me toward the airlock, past the Guards. They salute him as we pass.

At the airlock door, I have my Link scan all the seals and the air quality within the hangar. It comes back perfect, and I open the airlock, stepping into the hangar. My feet beat a steady path toward Sparrow, forsaking the passenger ship sitting beyond her.

But Ricardo's hand slips from mine.

I turn around, only to find his jaw moving, mouth working soundlessly.

350

"What's wrong?"

He stares at me, clearly searching for words. "I… I don't know how to ask this…"

"So, just ask."

"Have you… I mean…" He stares at the floor for a moment and pulls in a deep breath. Lifting his gaze, he looks at Sparrow, then finally looks back to me. "Have you had anything to drink?"

Shame burns my cheeks, coloring me scarlet. My gaze falls to the floor, and I shake my head. "No," I say. "I don't fly drunk. That'd be irresponsible. Besides, I don't need to."

I turn around, letting my Link lower Sparrow's hatch. Ducking into the darkness of her hull, I wipe a stray tear away, scurrying from his view.

Of course, he's worried I'll fly us into the side of the hangar and drop the station out of orbit…

Why wouldn't he worry about that?

But he surprises me, climbing aboard behind me.

"What do you mean, you 'don't need to' fly drunk?"

I move through the cargo bay, then up into the cockpit. Taking my seat, I wait for Ricardo to sit in the co-pilot seat. My Link triggers the turntable, raises the hatch, and shuts down the airlock.

As the hangar door opens, showing me heaven, I say, "Have you ever found that one place where you just feel okay? Like... Nothing has changed, your life is just as crappy, but you just *feel* better?"

I lean forward, craning my neck to see the tiny sliver of space visible beneath the slowly opening door. "I talked to Cait about it a long time ago. She thinks it's a control thing because there are so many things that have to be perfect when flying. She also thought it might be because there's enough to do on Sparrow to actually occupy my mind." I shake my head, exhaling softly.

"Flying is just... part of me. It's reflex and muscle memory." I run a loving hand over the edge of a control panel, noting a little scuff from a repair job three years ago.

I got so mad at Lachlan over that.

"I've been flying since I was a kid, not that I was supposed to. Those first couple of flights were sketchy," I say with a chuckle.

Ricardo laughs, pulling my attention from Sparrow for a heartbeat. Turning to face the vast expanse of space now visible through the open door, I say, "Even when I'm just sitting here, or if I float Sparrow out there and stare off toward Earth, I just feel better. Next to all the atrocities on Earth, my own failings aren't so bad. Next to the universe, my problems don't seem so big. It just... humbles me. It gives me hope that maybe somewhere out there… Maybe there's somewhere better. And maybe I'll get to see it. I just have to stick around."

Painful as that prospect might be, sometimes.

Glancing at Ricardo, I say, "Steady yourself."

He tips his head in confusion, but buckles himself in.

I don't bother with my restraints. I shut off the artificial gravity in Sparrow and in the hangar, letting the locks on our landing gear hold the ship down as I luxuriate in the feeling of weightlessness. As I drift slowly upward, I stare out at the wonders of space, watching stars blink and twinkle.

Ricardo unbuckles, drifting up beside me. We stare out at the stars, at the place where Earth must be, distant and broken. My arms float up before me. My hands tremble softly, drawing my attention, and I pull in a deep breath.

"I know I have a problem," I whisper. "I can see my hands shaking just as well as you all can. I crossed a line."

A lump forms in my throat, and I hate the way I cut up what I've done, transforming it into four little words. *I crossed a line.* It seems so trite, so much of an understatement that it doesn't deserve to be spoken. "I just… I couldn't stand to think."

Ricardo reaches for my shaking hand, wrapping it in his. "Olivia, you know I'm here for you, if you need anything. Just stick around, okay?"

But his voice breaks.

And it cracks me wide open.

"I'm sorry," I whisper. Tears float free of my eyes. With my free hand, I catch them up, smearing them over my shirt lest they find their way into a control panel.

"I know," Ricardo says.

He pulls me toward him, wrapping his arms around me, and I turn from the stars to weep into his chest.

Chapter Forty
Odyssey Space Research Station

Ricardo

We wander back to Olivia's room with hands linked. Darkness fills the halls. Soft emergency lights offer up just enough of a glow for us to see where we need to go.

Olivia's tears yet stain my shirt, and the tracks of a couple new ones shine on her face. I squeeze her hand, aching to make her feel better. A light tremor shakes her fingers against mine, but it's nothing compared to the shakes that rattled her mere days ago.

Every day without a drink, she gets better.

My mind drifts over all that we've been through in our short time together, all that our families put us through and all they did to the Regonians.

All the things they paid for.

The execution drifts through my mind, the deaths that I didn't have the stomach to watch. While my brother died, while electricity tore through Olivia's mother, we packed up Olivia's things.

Was that wrong?

Should I have watched?

My stomach churns, and my heart twists in my chest. But I know I've already gone over this.

I'll watch as he's jettisoned. That's it.

Despite my resolution, I'm filled with the morbid need to ask for the footage of his execution, for some sort of closure. But I know I'll find none.

Not in that footage.

Not in his release into space.

Not in the memory of my last conversation with him.

Again, his voice floats through my head, answering my only question. "Because this is war," he sneered at me. "Do you know what kind of people win wars, big brother? People who do what needs done."

A sickening wave of disgust and hatred burn through me, making me wonder where the little boy I tried so hard to protect went. I rub my free hand over my face and try not to think about it.

But the look on his face comes back, over and over. Hard and angular, he didn't even look like the plump little boy from our youth.

How long was it since the last time I saw him? Six, seven months?

How long since I sat in the same room and talked to him for more than a minute? A year and a half?

But he's an adult. His choices are his own.

Or at least, they were.

I sigh as we round the last corner, turning toward Olivia's room. Tenna's old room lies vacant with the door firmly closed. I stare at it as we pass, hoping she, Krona, and the remains of Daen Tribe are faring well on Venice.

Or at least, as well as can be expected.

Olivia's door slides open, welcoming us in, but with all the fabrics taken down and most of her stuff packed away, it isn't quite so cozy as before. Warm light envelops us as the door slides shut behind us.

She releases my hand, resting her weight against the wall as she pulls off her shoes.

But I look around at the things left unpacked.

A book with a girl's face on the cover, silver shining around her iris. A few baubles I haven't asked her about, yet. A little block of a 'phone,' a primitive Link of sorts, with the word 'Nokia' proudly emblazoned below the tiny screen.

All these things sit, waiting to be stowed away and carried off to a new home. All my stuff rests in a suitcase tucked under her bed, so paltry in comparison to the things she's collected.

Music whispers into existence. "This is the One by David O'Dowda. 2016" flashes across my Link.

Slender arms slide around my waist, and Olivia presses her lips against my back. Turning to face her, I wrap my arms around her. Butterflies erupt in my stomach. I ache to kiss her, but with everything going on, with how long it's been since we shared that sort of intimacy, does she even want that from me?

My eyes fall to her lips, tracing the sensuous curves. Breathing hard, I lean closer, lifting my gaze to meet hers.

And I stop in my tracks.

A tear slips over her cheek, and she falters. Wiping it away, she stares at my chest.

Pulling in a deep breath, I tuck her against me, cradling the back of her head.

"I wish we could just start over," she whispers.

A lance of pain pierces my heart.

I pull back, sliding my hand beneath her chin and tipping her head back. She meets my eyes, but only for a moment.

"If we started over," I say, hating even the thought, "if we pretend none of this happened, I wouldn't know how smart and strong and resilient you are."

She stares up at me, brows scrunched and eyes welling up.

"Sure, I'd know how beautiful you are, so of course I'd *want* to get to know you, but…" I shake my head, trailing off. With a sigh, I continue, "I know things have been difficult."

I shake my head again.

A few more tears fall over Olivia's cheeks.

"I don't want to start over though. I like knowing you. I don't want to pretend that I don't."

Olivia's lips part. She searches my face, eyes roaming restlessly. Finally, she holds my gaze, nodding slowly.

The song shifts, moving into the soft piano of "Arcanine by Ursine Vulpine. 2017" as I wait for her to speak, to move, to do something.

Anything.

And I don't have to wait long.

Rising onto tiptoes, she brushes her lips against mine. Her hands slide into my hair, tangling into fists, and she pulls me tight against her.

And I react, hungry and aching. I taste her, feel her. My hands grip her hips, her hair. I nip at her bottom lip. Need consumes us, and we rip our clothes away. They fall in heaps around us, leaving me to revel in her bare skin.

Desperate, I push her back against the door, moving against her, grasping her buttocks, delighting in her soft moan. Our mouths dance together, hot and burning. She trails a hand over my spine, sending shivers through me.

And the ache builds.

Grasping her thighs, I lift her, pinning her against the door. She braces herself with arms wrapped around me and hands gripping tight.

A crushing kiss earns me another moan, and I tense, near to bursting.

Sliding home, I plunge inside her, loving the delicate heat, the sweetness of her. She kisses my neck, sending shockwaves through me, and I move within her, pushing, pulsing. Aching, we climb higher, grinding together in a dance older than this place, older than the travesties we've known, older than time.

Her nails dig into my shoulders as her head tips back. Arching against me she gasps, hips moving in time with mine, grinding against me. Her body tenses around me, and she cries out, voice breaking over my name as she unravels in my arms.

I move faster, kissing her lips, her neck, anything I can reach, until I crumble.

Chapter Forty One
Odyssey Space Research Station

Olivia

I sit on the edge of my bed, fidgeting with the old comms unit. The black sphere rolls from one palm to the other and back again as a million questions spiral in my brain.

But how can I ask them? How can I start this conversation, this thing I've wanted for twelve years?

Ricardo rolls over behind me, and the sheets rustle beneath his questing hand. Eventually, he bumps my backside.

A groggy moan eases past his lips, and I look over my shoulder at him. Tousled hair riots all around his head, but he pushes it back from his eyes to meet my gaze. The soft light plays on his collarbones, casting delicate shadows into the hollows behind them.

Scrunching his brows, voice thick with sleep, he says, "What's wrong?"

I sigh, gripping the comms unit. I shake my head and hold it up for him to see. "I just…"

Again, I try to think of how to start this conversation, hating the circumstances that brought it about, the circumstances I have to explain and ask about, the things I have to try to gain from this relationship for the sake of humanity.

Even now that I can have my Dad back, he isn't mine.

I turn away from Ricardo, hiding the tears that prick at the corners of my eyes. The sink shines in the soft light, the only bright spot in the bathroom, but all I can think of is the alcohol I dumped down the drain and how much easier this conversation would be if I had a bit to drink.

Will Dad even want anything to do with me once he knows what I've become?

I sigh, barely noticing the shuffling of sheets behind me as Ricardo moves. His feet appear on either side of me, and he touches my waist.

"Come here," he whispers.

Turning, I find him propped against the wall with his knees drawn up.

"Come on," he says. "Talk to me."

A tear falls, and my heart lurches.

But I nod.

Setting the comms unit on the bed, I crawl back and sit between Ricardo's legs. He wraps his arms around me, leaning his head on mine when I recline against his bare chest. The scent of him, his touch, warms me. And for a few moments, I let myself soak it in, waiting for the tears to subside.

He presses a gentle kiss to the top of my head and asks, "Are you nervous?"

I nod slowly, then say, "What's to be nervous about? Telling my Dad how much of a disappointment I am? Hanging the fate of humanity on a weird Drennar? Or maybe the whole bit where I haven't heard from him in twelve years and just kind of assumed he was dead?"

My sarcasm earns me a chuckle.

"You're not a disappointment. And you can handle all the rest of that stuff," Ricardo says. "I'd be nervous filming a message in the nude though. Luckily, that's pretty easy to remedy."

Despite myself, I laugh. "I wasn't going to film it yet." I shake my head and roll my eyes, but I lean down to kiss the arm wrapped around my shoulders, resting atop my breasts. Sighing, dropping the levity, I add, "I was just trying to figure out how to…" I shrug. "I don't know what to say."

"Well, I can help you figure it out. If you want."

I nod. "Thank you. And…" I start, but relying on him, relying on anyone, just isn't my strong suit. My mouth goes dry, and I swallow hard.

I have to be better. I can't be the way I was.

So, I force myself to say, "Will you stay with me when I film it?"

Again, he presses full lips to the top of my head. "Gladly."

Chapter Forty Two
Novay

Reginald

Rone leads me down the hall, wings fluttering anxiously behind her in tight little twitches. A knot forms in my stomach. She knows, or at least has an idea, what the other Drennar have in store for me today. And if she's nervous, it can't be good.

Picking up my pace, I catch up, careful not to be smacked by a jittery wing. I wrap my hand around hers, lacing our fingers together.

After all, the others already know about us. Why keep hiding?

She glances at me and gives me a sad smile. "I don't know what they're going to show you, today," she says. "But they *are* showing you something, and considering the things they've shown you before..."

She trails off, and I give her hand a squeeze. Nodding, I turn to face the wall I know she'll transform into a door in a moment. My mind whirls, a veritable maelstrom of destruction and death, and my stomach sinks.

What else has Eva wrought? What more could she have done?

The Drennar seem to have made me their guinea pig in understanding depression and deprivation. So, a small part of me hopes they never show me Olivia.

If it means she can have a good life, one they can't torture me with, I hope I never see her face on their screen again.

Before parting the wall for us, Rone turns to me and says, "If this is bad... I'm sorry."

"You're not responsible for this," I whisper.

"Not anymore." Her brows furrow, but she parts the wall before I can say another word.

I steal my gaze from her, peering into the same room I've visited every day for 12 years. But it isn't the same room anymore. The small room with a Drennar in every corner now encompasses three times as much space, having been extended outward on either side.

In the new space, Drennar sit in rows, facing inward, staring at us. The sides of all their heads have been shaved to match Rone's, and their faces contort with anxiety and excitement.

I close my mouth, swallow, and take my place in one of two chairs in the center of the room facing a blank wall. Rone sits down next to me, glancing at the Drennar gathered around us. Vaguely, I recognize one as the man who found us out, the man Rone convinced they couldn't truly understand humans without emotion. Lustran.

The same Drennar that pulled me from my home all those years ago.

My heart gallops in my chest, faltering every so often. My palms sweat.

But so do Rone's.

She wipes her free hand on her pants, and squeezes tightly with the other, gripping my hand.

The stark, white light dims, fading near to nothingness, and my pulse quickens. Surrounded by unstable aliens, any one of which could snap me in half on a whim, about to be subjected to God knows what emotions, things they've only just begun to fathom...

I don't particularly like my odds.

The wall before me glows, and my heart lodges itself in my throat. The auditorium on Termana appears on the wall, but lines of white run through it. Entire vertical sections flicker and go black. Bits and pieces drop out of focus, then come back, and a great crackling sound surrounds me.

What the...

I lean forward, as though that might somehow make this mess of an image clearer. My brows furrow, and I try to piece together what I'm seeing.

People file into the auditorium, but the image cuts in half. The bottom half jerks to the side, misaligning the people and chairs.

"What is this?" Rone whispers.

But I have no answer. I've never seen footage so mangled and broken before.

I shake my head, watching as the top and bottom halves of the image reconnect, but shifted to the side, showing only half of the auditorium.

The seats fill with Humans, and then another door opens, admitting the survivors of Eva's wrath. The aliens file through the door, pouring in to fill the other half of the auditorium. A haze of white dots drifts across the screen, followed by large black patches, obscuring three aliens here, twenty there.

After they take their seats, the Coalition takes the stage, minus two members. Guards and Soldiers lead the accused, or in this case, the guilty, into the seats that butt up against the stage.

My eyes pick her out of the crowd easily, showing me a version of the woman I married, aged by exhaustion and her own cruelty. But she isn't the woman I knew, the woman I loved. She isn't the woman I wanted to spend all my years with.

My mouth goes dry.

Rone squeezes my hand, reminding me that I'm not alone. Not like Eva is.

As a rogue wave of static overwhelms half the screen, I wonder if I would've done what she did if she'd offered herself up in Olivia's place, if she'd left me behind.

But I know I wouldn't.

As much as I used to love her, she always loved me more. And I couldn't have done that to Olivia.

I would've done right by our daughter, done better than Eva.

Not that it would've taken much to be better.

Bitterness wells within me, and fury riots in my veins. My free hand curls into a fist. I grip Rone's hand, careful not to squeeze too hard, though I doubt I could hurt her.

I pull in a deep breath, trying to calm myself.

The screen goes black for a moment, then the auditorium reappears. But the timestamp jumps forward a few hours. Static hisses at the edges, and a soft crackle overlays the audio.

I furrow my brows.

What's going on?

Standing proud, two Regonians, including the one I saw in the crate, rise to their feet. The woman addresses those gathered for the tribunal, but only a few words come through the lingering static.

Slowly, more and more of her words come through. I lean forward, straining my ears to pick out the meaning between the crackles.

"...all those... these depraved..." The Regonian woman's face shifts, deadly serious. The static parts, as if intimidated by her. "I. Demand. Death. No one slaughters my people and lives. Either you order their death, or I will."

Chills run down my spine, and I swallow.

Beside this woman, this leader, three Regonians rise and stomp their feet. Beside 0001, apparently her partner, still more rise, stomping three times.

All around me, the newly emotional Drennar sit forward in their seats or fidget anxiously. They shift and whisper excitedly.

Three bands of black stripe the screen as the rest of the survivors rise behind their leaders, pounding the floor with heavy beats. Fear shines in the eyes of every Human in the auditorium that isn't obscured by black patches and static.
376

My heart pounds against my ribs, and Rone sits still, riveted to the spot. But on all sides, feelings overwhelm the Drennar. One weeps, another begins to stomp in time with the Regonians.

"Please..." I beg.

But what should I hope for?

The execution of the woman I once loved? Certainly not the death of innocents when the Regonians seek revenge if her death isn't ordered.

A wave of static consumes the screen before I can piece myself together. The wall goes black, plunging the room into darkness. An ethereal glow emanates from the wall as another transmission takes shape.

But the oddity of the static gnaws at me.

"Wait..." I say, staring at one of the Drennar in the corners, one of the unshaven, unmodified guards. "What was wrong with that footage?"

The Drennar have never shown me anything so... broken.

"Your daughter was working on a defense program in her spare time. She enabled it, but it does not seem to have gone to plan," the Drennar tells me, tone even and face expressionless.

My jaw falls open. Shock rasps through me, and I shake my head. "What do you mean?"

He meets my gaze, but only to send fans of light outward, analyzing me as he says, "All their security systems have been compromised. Video and audio surveillance is corrupted. Airlock doors are sealed in emergency lock downs. Those on Termana will be fine. Those in orbit have only a limited food supply."

My blood runs cold, and I breathe a sigh of guilty relief, knowing that if Olivia is in that auditorium, she's on Termana.

She's safe.

Tears prick at the corners of my eyes.

"We pulled back to see how they handle the situation. This stands to be informative. Humans are skilled at making trouble for themselves," the same Drennar says, concluding his fan analysis.

That we are...

But I'm left no more time to worry. The screen bursts to life, a discordant array of movement amidst black and white dots. A deafening blast of hissing and crackling blares through the room, and I jerk my hands up to cover my ears.

Amidst rainbow bursts and stripes of black, a lab tech straps Eva to a bed. Electrodes stick to her with wires hanging from them, bundled at the end to a single connector.

The tech plugs them in with trembling hands. He fetches a sedative block from a tray next to him and places it on the inside of Eva's elbow. Fingering the button atop it, he swallows, holding Eva's gaze.

The hissing static intensifies as he presses the button, engaging the needle and injecting the sedative. His shoulders rise and fall, far too quickly.

My mouth goes dry, and my free hand comes up to cover the bottom half of my face.

But Eva merely sucks in her lips.

Half covered by static, the tech removes the sedative block, dropping it into a bin on the tray. It's the first one he's used, but it won't be the last. A lever raises Eva's bed higher into the air, passing her image through a multicolor splotch on the screen, and a Guard escorts another person to the stack of beds beneath her.

But Eva reappears on the other side of the corrupted patch of video, brows furrowed and eyes closed, and I seek her out. The woman I would have fought to save twelve years ago. Five years ago.

A few months ago.

I close my eyes, and images of her attack on Odyssey flicker through my mind, followed by the dream of her killing me with Olivia lying dead on a gurney next to me, dead by

Eva's hand. In my mind, I watch her condemn Olivia, our beautiful daughter, to die in the lab alongside the Regonian fighters.

Rage boils within me, tensing every muscle in my body.

I open my eyes, jaw clenched and teeth grinding together, desperate for an outlet for this fury. But the woman on the screen looks so small, so feeble. White dots vibrate on the screen, half-concealing her, but she's there.

And she doesn't look like someone who could kill 2,000 people.

She doesn't look like a monster.

Her hands ball into fists, grasping the sides of her loose hospital gown, and she winces, drawing my eyes to the place where her Link once rested, now reclaimed to be refurbished. Gauze decorates her skin in more places than I can name tech for.

"Oh, Eva…" I whisper. "What have you done?"

My heart twists, contorting in agony. I shake my head slowly.

A single tear slips free of her eyes, once such a warm brown, but now… Now, they've lost their shine, their light. Staring straight up, she pulls in a deep breath. Her eyes close, and she mouths a single word.

The static blaring all around me muffles the sound, but I know the word. How many times did I watch her lips form it in our time together?

But seeing my name on her lips now…

Guilt seeps into me, churning in my stomach, because I know she did this for me.

So many people dead… For me.

Olivia's childhood ruined… For me.

Her own life, burdened and stunted and broken, soon to be over.

For me.

A sob shakes the room, and I jump. A Drennar off to my left weeps openly. But my gaze doesn't linger long, doesn't try to find the tears amidst a crowd of strangers.

Staring at the screen, I watch Eva's breathing even out as the sedative kicks in. Black spots expand, slowly spreading over the screen. As Eva's bed rises higher and higher, getting closer to the camera, as more people are loaded into the beds beneath her, the spots of darkness trail behind, reaching for her. Slowly, they conceal her from view.

In the corner of the screen, a tech approaches a control panel. Three others stand nearby with Links poised to scan in.

They hold their Links up to the panel, placing their free hands on sensors.

The hissing ceases, but the black spots spread, consuming nearly everything. A few patches of Washington Station remain unobscured, showing a hand here, a foot there. The last tech places their hand on their sensor, and the air fills with the chaos of flailing limbs and shaking beds. Flashes of twitching body parts come in and out of view in the little spots of visibility.

She's gone.

My jaw falls open.

I should cry, I should shout.

I should feel *something.*

But a deep numbness settles over me, chilling my heart. The screen fades to black, then shifts into its normal steely-gray color. Light floods the room, blinding me, but I stare straight ahead.

Unmoving.

Unblinking.

Emptiness spreads within me, erasing everything. But it could never erase enough. Everything I've done, everything I hoped for, everything I wanted for Olivia and Eva… It's all come crashing down.

I drop my gaze, staring at the floor.

All around me, Drennar crumble beneath emotions they've never felt before.

Rone rises to her feet. Standing before me, she tugs on my hand. I look up at her, at the blue striations in her green eyes, at her short black hair and the wings unfurled behind her.

At the compassion shining in her eyes.

She pulls me to my feet and wraps her arms around me. Blinking rapidly, I wrap my arms around her waist and bury my face in the side of her neck.

Her hand finds the back of my head, cradling me to her as she whispers, "I'm sorry."

***

Lying awake in my bed, nestled against Rone's chest in the darkness, I try not to think about what I saw today. I try not to think about Eva's death or the Regonians she killed. I try not to think of the ceremony the Drennar showed me afterward, of the dancing and chanting and singing that took place amidst the surviving Regonians. I try not to think of the silence that fell over them when the time came for Eva's death.

Rone pulls back and touches my face. A smile parts her lips, and she whispers, "Do you want some good news?"

I stare at her, struggling to find anything that might be considered good in all the worlds, something that might reasonably come into my life.

She doesn't wait for my answer. Leaning closer, she whispers, "I just got a message from Olivia."

The shell of numbness cracks and falls away. Tears cascade over my cheeks, overwhelming me. Gripping Rone, I pull her tighter to me, gasping for breath as sobs of relief wash through me.

She places her hands on my cheeks, staring into my eyes. Gently, she kisses my lips. "Do you want to see her message? Or do you need a minute?"

I shake my head vehemently. "No, I want to see it. I want to see her, to know she's okay."

My tears flow freely, and a few glitter in Rone's eyes, barely visible in the near-darkness.

"Okay," she says, voice thick with emotion. "Come on."

She sits up, draping her legs over the side of the bed. Her wings rustle, sweeping over the pillows. I sit up, staring at the wall before me with my hands steepled and pressed against my face.

Rone works some magic with the tech, somehow ensuring a private connection, and I prepare myself for static and blotches and blacked out spots concealing parts of Olivia.

But the wall glows with the pristine image of my daughter.

I gasp, and tears fall in earnest. Pale and struggling for words, there she is. My little girl.

A few tears fall from her eyes, mirroring my own. A man rubs her back gently, but I only notice him because she looks at him before speaking.

"Dad…" Olivia whispers, soft brown eyes filling to the brim with tears. She wipes them away, but more come to take their place immediately.

A sob chokes me, rattling my frame.

"Dad, I've missed you… So much."

"I'm so sorry, baby," I whisper, choking on my words even though she can't hear me.

Olivia weeps, wrapping her arms around herself. The man with her pulls her close, stroking her hair and kissing the top of her forehead.

"It's okay," he whispers as she cries against his chest.

My heart constricts, and my breath hitches. Rone rubs a gentle hand over my back.

Slowly, Olivia sits back up, facing her camera. Tears stain her cheeks, and still more fall. She opens her mouth to speak, and my heart stops.

"I don't even know where to start…" Her gaze falls, staring at whatever her camera rests upon. "Everything is just…"

Her lips purse, and her eyes well up again, pulling sympathetic tears from my own eyes.

"Everything is so messed up," she whimpers. Pulling in a great gulp of breath, she shudders beneath the weight she's carried. "I just don't know… I don't know what I could've done to stop her. And I failed. I let so many people down."

The man with my daughter rushes in to comfort her as I collapse into tears and despair. The video continues to play, and eventually Olivia speaks again.

My sobs drown out her words, and I know I'll ask Rone to play it again, as many times as she'll oblige me.

Chapter Forty Three
Venice Space Research Station

Krona

I smile as I hang a bar down the center of our room, securing it to a beam in the ceiling, careful to split the window evenly. Tenna brings me a stack of tapestries, special deliveries from Olivia. My heart glows as I hang them. The newest members of our Tribe, of our family, will join us soon.

As my hands work, attaching tapestries to the bar, I let my mind wander, trying to pinpoint the exact moment when Olivia and Ricardo became a part of our family.

Maybe when Ricardo broke me out of that cell? Or when Olivia agreed to seek justice on our behalf?

Or when that deranged man attacked her?

Or maybe in a million smaller moments?

Try as I might, I can't figure it out. I take a deep breath and shake my head, smiling.

One way or another, they're Daen Tribe, now.

I hang the last tapestry and step back to analyze my work. Tenna moves beyond them, but the thick, heavy fabrics show no silhouettes. They muffle the sound of her steps, but a bit of sound passes over them, squeezing through where open air breathes between the bar and the beam.

Soft footsteps trod across the floor, barely audible, and I slide a tapestry aside to allow Tenna passage. I watch the sinuous muscles ripple in her legs as she lifts the bed, letting my eyes trail over her strong physique. She carries the Human-sized thing to Ricardo and Olivia's side with ease, meeting my gaze with a smile as she passes.

Knowing how much work remains, fully aware of the affect her backside and firm legs will have on me, I tear my eyes away from her before she lowers the bed. I leave the tapestries slid aside, and turn to face our bedding, piled high on the window bench. Spreading it out on the floor, I find myself wishing for the soft fabrics of our own bed on Regonia.

But when Tenna presses up against my back, sliding her arms around my waist, I know the bedding doesn't matter as long as we're together.

Our time apart, split up by Human experimentation, flits through my mind in the form of a stone cell on a space station in the Realm of Stars. But Tenna scatters those thoughts to the far ends of the space. Her lips find my neck, my ear. Slowly, she slides her hand beneath my shirt, letting her fingers play low on my stomach.

A soft moan escapes me. I close my eyes, savoring her touch and figuring out how long we have before Olivia and Ricardo get here.

Just long enough.

Her hand slides downward, plunging beneath the waistband of my pants. She moves her hand over me just how I like, cupping and stroking, teasing me.

My heart races, and my lungs work in shallow bursts.

She pulls her hand free, then pushes my shirt up over my torso, trailing her fingertips over my skin. I rip the cursed fabric over my head and toss it away, grateful for the freedom its absence allows her.

She traces a scar on my ribs with one finger, slides her tongue over another on my spine. Her hands desert me, but I shudder as she kisses my neck again. Something soft falls to the floor, and she presses bare breasts against my back.

A deep, guttural groan rumbles through me, but she leaves me no time to turn around, to join with her. Her hands find me, unfastening my pants with ease. She lets them fall, and before I can kick them away, she takes me in her grip once more, torturing me with slow movements.

Reaching behind me, I grasp her hip, pressing her against me. But my body aches, begging me for more. Slipping my hands between us, I undo her pants and let my hands slide over firm thighs to push the garment down.

She bites my shoulder and grips me tighter, barely masking a sweet moan.

Turning, I press my lips to hers, reveling in the feel of her hands sliding up and over my chest, tangling into my hair. I wrap one arm around her waist, holding tight, and use the other to caress the sensitive skin of her stomach, trailing downward.

Warmth greets my questing fingers, and her breathing hitches. I move deftly, working her to a fever pitch, and she clings to me. Our breaths come hot and heavy, fast and desperate. Her nails carve into my back, and I groan, craving more.

I lay her down on our freshly spread bedding and kiss her lips. I taste her neck and ravage her breasts, then move lower, showering her stomach with kisses.

My hands grasp her buttocks, her thighs. Aching for her, I kiss the firm muscles, then bite the delicate skin of her inner thigh.

She squirms for me, breathing heavily. "Krona," she whispers, and I know the time has come.

She pulls me up, kissing me hungrily, and I plunge inside her. Desperately, we move together, mouths dancing in a feverish union all the while.

I touch her neck, and her heart gallops beneath my palm, beating just as fast as my own. My body tenses, aching sweetly, and I let my fingers trail over Tenna's honed physique, pushing her further and further toward release.

She cries out, arching her back and pressing her breasts against me. She shudders, sending ripples of delicate agony writhing through me.

My body burns, but I slow my pace, drag it out. She arches, tense around me, and my fingers find their mark. She unravels once more, nails digging into my back.

Driving home one last time, holding her mossy gaze, I shatter within her. She tastes my lips, hands twisting in my hair.

"Hoo kai voo mai," she whispers, words taking on stronger meaning after finding her brother's sound.

"Hoo kai voo mai," I say, breathless.

I kiss her, wanting to make sure she knows. Our time apart, separated by stars and cruel experiments, seeps back into my memory, and I kiss her again.

But my arms shake beneath me. I collapse beside her, trembling and panting.

She rolls to face me sliding one leg over me. Her fingers trace my collarbone and the scar that crosses it. She finds another and another, kissing each with tender attention.

So many scars, so many battles, and the worst is yet to come.

Tenna deserts my chest and kisses my lips, sweet and delicate. I smile, grateful to face the rest of my days by her side, however many I may have left.

Chapter Forty Four
Novay

Reginald

My stomach ties itself in knots as I settle into the chair in my testing room. Rone sits beside me, instantly taking my hand in hers. On either side, Drennar sit in rows, muttering nervously, wearing their new emotions on their sleeves.

Their chatter only serves to fray my nerves, lending the frantic pacing of my heart a background of whispers and breaking voices. I drum the fingers of my free hand on my lap, waiting, dreading whatever might appear before me.

Lights flicker on the ears of the Drennar in the corners, the only sign that they aren't statues. They stare at us, unblinking. Their arms hang at their sides.

My eyes dart from one to another, wondering how they can be so still, how they can stand by as they prepare another attempt to break me.

I turn in my seat, peeking at a Drennar in the back corner. His unusually dark skin, nearly black, shines in the bright lights. Two of his six arms rest behind his elongated torso, clasped out of the way. The other four hang idle. Lights flicker behind his eyes, sending patterns through the clear plate in the side of his skull to dance upon the wall. He tips his head to the side, regarding me.

A deep sickness creeps into my gut as I turn to face the wall in front of me.

Why are they waiting?

Why won't they just show me and get it over with?

Slowly, the room dims, stealing the Drennar around me from my sight. Three little flickers of light pierce the darkness to my left as one of them receives a transmission. It blinks out, plunging us all into inky darkness, and my heart stutters.

I gulp down a breath, clinging to Rone's hand.

What is it this time?

Static hisses through the air, and I jump. The wall before me morphs, and a dull glow fills the room, marred by dark splotches shifting over the wall. Vertical lines of ever-changing colors pierce the black patches, but the cockpit of a ship takes shape behind the distortions.

Olivia drops down into the pilot seat.

My heart lurches, dreading whatever might come next. I grip the arm of my chair, and the metal digs into my palm.

They only show me terrible things...

Please, please... Let her be okay.

Bits and pieces of sorrowful music weep out between bursts of static, and tears pour over Olivia's cheeks. The view out the front window shifts as she spins the ship and opens the hangar door.

Black spots flicker over the screen, colliding and consuming the bottom half. But Olivia's face shines in the dim light, slick with tears. Staring out at the heavens, she pulls in a deep breath.

And so do I.

Rone's free hand comes to rest atop our interwoven fingers. I lean forward, desperate for things to go well.

Maybe they fixed some of the problems with her program. The hangar door opened, after all.

Maybe they just want me to see that she fixed part of it, that she's going on a supply run.

But she's not wearing a flight suit.

And her tears keep falling.

Her body shifts, and her face falls, looking at something in her hands, something I can't see. She looks back up at the stars, stealing my breath away as she whispers, "Keep me with you..."

Her words reach out of the static to breathe an eerie chill over my spine. My stomach turns over, and my heart plummets.

The darkness recedes from the bottom of the screen, shifting to fill only the corners. Bright white lines dance over the wall.

And Olivia lifts a handful of pills.

"Oh my god…"

My heart fractures as she gulps them down, washing them away with the contents of a small brown bottle.

"No, Olivia, please…"

My voice breaks, and tears fall freely.

Olivia's Link glows a warm amber, and she stares at it for a moment. Then, she lifts another handful of pills to her mouth. She drains the little brown bottle, and a hollow clank pierces the static.

I slide from my chair, crumpling into a shuddering heap on the floor. Every fiber of my being aches to save her, to spare her all the pain she's felt, but these fucking Drennar have me on a different planet.

Rone sniffles in her chair, and those lining the walls sob openly as Olivia closes her eyes.

"I'm sorry dad," she whispers. "I should've been so much better."

The world falls out from under me. I desert Rone's hand, crawling forward on hands and knees. I reach out, touching the wall, touching Olivia's limp hand hanging beside her chair.

"No, baby," I croak. "You couldn't have been better. You're all you should've been. Just please, please don't do this. Please!"

I crumble, leaning against the wall and staring at my daughter's slack form. Tears blur my vision, and the image splits, tearing Olivia in two.

On the wall, the man from her message barges into the cockpit, followed by Guards. Shock holds him still, but only for an instant.

My heart falters, and I fall silent.

"Please, please save her. Please!" I scream the last word, needing my voice to carry through time and space to urge this man to move faster, to be there for Olivia like I can't be.

But dark circles expand on the wall, covering his rescue attempt and stealing my daughter from my sight.

The wall shifts, becoming its usual steel grey. The lights come on, blinding me.

"NOOO!"

I pound my fists against the wall, screaming until my voice breaks. Tears wash over my face in great torrents, and my heart shatters within my chest.

Shoving myself up from the ground, I charge the six-armed Drennar in the nearest corner. "Bring her back!" I scream, pounding my fists against his expansive chest.

He doesn't move, doesn't flinch.

"We need you to take your seat. We have some equations for you to do," he says, cold and emotionless. The Drennar seated on the edges of the room gasp.

"You expect me to do fucking math after... after seeing Olivia..."

A sob chokes me, and my heart freezes. But my fists hit harder, pummeling this beast, this robot.

Rone rushes up behind me, wrapping strong arms around my waist. She tears me away from him, carefully dodging my flailing arms and legs.

"NO! Let me go! Please, just bring her back!"

"Reginald!" Rone demands, turning me around to face her.

402

Tears streak her cheeks, sticking strands of hair to her pale grey skin. Red rims her eyes. The pieces of my heart twist in my chest, stabbing me with brittle edges.

She pulls me close, wrapping me in a tight embrace. With a hand on the back of my head, she tucks my face against her neck. Soft sounds caress my ear, but it takes me a moment to realize she's making words, not just sounds.

Barely audible, she whispers, "Look at the dates."

A message from her pops into my head, somehow circumventing the glowing alert on my Link. Two images, still frames. One from the horror they've just shown me, one from the message from Olivia.

My heart explodes as I see the dates of the recordings side by side, the little numbers that suddenly mean everything.

She's alive!

He saved her!

My knees buckle, and Rone crumples, going to the floor with me. Her embrace tightens as sobs rattle through me. My hand tangles in her hair, pulling her closer.

Blue fans of light sweep over us, over the rest of the room.

And all around me, Drennar weep openly, begging to know what happened to Olivia.

For their own sake.

And for mine.

***

I drag myself through the hall, clinging to Rone's hand. My gaze never rises from the cold floor at my feet. Exhausted, my face hangs slack and emotionless.

Without a word, she opens the passage to my room, and we step through. I stand there, too broken to move.

Rone tugs at my hand, trying to convince me to have a seat.

But I can't.

I can't move, can't even bear to be here.

Chapter Forty Five
Novay

Rone

At long last, Reginald sits on his bed. He curls into himself, drawing his feet up and tucking his knees against his chest. I linger near the door, chest collapsing, surprising me with the ferocity of the pain caused by emotion.

Logic demands that I escape this room. My brain warns against getting wrapped up with him any further, falling away from my own people, as it has warned me so many times in the past.

But my heart lurches at the prospect of leaving.

And my people are the reason he's breaking.

So, I crawl onto the bed, sitting behind him and letting my legs fall on either side of him. I wrap my arms around him, and he falls back against me.

He weeps openly, because even though he knows now that Olivia survived her suicide attempt, the sight of it, the thought of it eats away at him.

Just as it eats away at me.

My mind whirls, trying to process the effects these emotions are having on me. My heart crumbles beneath their weight.

And horror spreads through me at all my species has done.

How can we do this?

How did we ever think we had a right to do this?

All the experiments, here and on other planets, flash through my mind, dreadful slide shows of what now looks a lot like torture. I swallow back a lump in my throat as sobs rack Reginald's body.

We're monsters.

Images of Olivia chasing one poison with another, alone on a spaceship, flood me. My mind fills with this aching girl who would've been happy if not for us.

Reginald nestles closer, reclining against me, and despite everything, my heart flutters. But a weight drops through me, pulling my stomach down to the floor beneath the bed.

How can I feel so happy to have him here? With everything that I've done, how can I think this is good?

Even now, even with emotion and regret... Am I still a monster?

I shrink from the horror, but my arms tighten around Reginald. My mind, my predisposition for logic sweeps in, analyzing the situation and rescuing me.

It tells me that if given the choice, if I'd known how it would hurt him, how it would hurt Olivia and the Regonians, if I'd truly understood then as I do now, I wouldn't have brought him here.

Realization sweeps through me, even as waves of fear try to suppress it. But I know what I have to do now, know the path I must walk.

And I've already begun the treasonous journey to save humanity from us.

I just have to finish it.

Continue reading in *Ascending*, book three of The Regonia Chronicles.

Thank you!

For buying this book. For reading it all the way through.

If you liked it, please leave a review on Amazon, Goodreads, Barnes & Noble, your blog... Anywhere, really. Reviews are the lifeblood of authors, helping books get noticed in the almighty eyes of search engine algorithms. Even if only a few words, a review is incredibly helpful.

Eager to stay up to date on the latest dark fiction from Elexis Bell?

Sign up for her newsletter.

Other Books by this Author

Literary Fantasy Novels

Soul Bearer

The Gem of Meruna

A Heart of Salt & Silver

Allmother Rising

Literary Thriller Novellas

Annabelle

Things Left Unsaid

Literary Post-Apocalyptic Novel

World for the Broken

About the Author

Elexis Bell is a quiet nerd with too many hobbies, including everything from gaming to shower-singing and even archery, weather permitting. She specializes in sarcasm and writing stories that make people feel. She's made a home for herself with her husband and a small army of cats.

She writes dark, gritty stories, sprinkling gut-wrenching emotions over high fantasy romance, thrillers, post-apocalyptic romance, and science fiction.

For further information, follow her on Instagram, Twitter, or Facebook, or check out her blog on her website. There, you can sign up for her newsletter to stay up to date on all future book releases, giveaways, and ongoing projects.

www.elexisbell.com